IMAGES OF DEATH

Sir Gregory Fortis, a former head of British Intelligence, dies near his home in Testem Magna after being torn to death by his Dobermann dogs. Weeks later, the village's local policeman is shot at with an Armalite rifle — hardly the weapon of a poacher. Two unusual events bring the Serious Incident Unit to the village to investigate the possibility of a connection. Sergeant Jack Bull heads the Unit, and has his own reasons for hoping for a straightforward arrest. But his hopes are soon dashed . . .

Books by Lawrence Williams
in the Linford Mystery Library:

THE MURDER TRIANGLE

LAWRENCE WILLIAMS

IMAGES OF DEATH

Complete and Unabridged

LINFORD
Leicester

Williams, Lawrence, *1915* –
    Images of death.—Large print ed.—
    Linford mystery library
    1. Detective and mystery stories
    2. Large type books
    I. Title
    813.5′4 [F]

    ISBN 1–84617–489–9

Published by
F. A. Thorpe (Publishing)
Anstey, Leicestershire

Set by Words & Graphics Ltd.
Anstey, Leicestershire
Printed and bound in Great Britain by
T. J. International Ltd., Padstow, Cornwall

This book is printed on acid-free paper

For Alistair who saw

Man is a creature of myths.[1] One of the most powerful of his myths is the existence of reality.

The exploration of this myth is a proper task for novelists working in the last years of this century. *The Legendary Murder Series* is one exploration. Appropriately, it also concerns itself with the myths of time and death.

---

[1] I use the word myth as defined by the novel *The White Hotel* written by D. M. Thomas. Only the landscapes are different.

1

A graveyard etched into a steel sky. Shapes are defined, colours leached away by dawn light. Gravestones, tilted and upright, are flecked with elderly snow cold-burned into stone, frozen into every engraved letter. The yews, the tufted grass of untrimmed paths, bear the same mean powdering of dust. It is too cold for soft, deep, red-robin snow. The only image that attests life is the grave. Heavy coating of night frost does not disguise the cakey mounds of turned earth standing almost warmly in the bitter scene. This irony is emphasized by the exceptional height of the mounds rising above a pit too deep for one coffin.

Now: the first life since first light. Two black swaddled figures enter left. There is barely time to perceive these black waddling crows before eye and mind are riveted on their burden. The men struggle, somewhat resentfully, with a

1

large canvas sack which they carry between them, one bearer walking ahead of the other. The sack is silver-grey, its contents indecipherably bulbous, floppy. The undertakers halt, allow the middle part of the sack to thump the frozen path. Impossible to tell whether they feel demeaned by the task or embarrassed by the weight, but the contents are not reverenced, are not trade goods.

Momentarily, the only movement is the exhalation of their breaths: white clouds that nudge their hat brims before vanishing. Then the man at the rear, the senior bearer, speaks. There is no sound; grip of winter has silenced the world. But whatever is said is understood by the younger man, and it increases his resentment. He releases hold completely, allows his half of the sack to flop down at his feet. He does not reply to his companion but, breath spurting before his face, angrily folds arms across chest, hugs the heavy black coat against himself. After a long pause the older man speaks again. The younger scowls, slowly unfurls himself, stoops down over their burden.

As he tries to raise his end of it the unevenly weighted sack lurches to his right. Both men grapple with it, feet splayed, muscles taut under the heavy cloth of their overcoats. As they adjust the weight, lift the sack, their black-hatted heads are slowly raised and silhouetted against the sky. This is the moment for watchers to note that the light is getting brighter but, instead, they must comprehend a new and disgusting image.

From the nose of the man in the rear, the older man, a black worm appears. The man is either oblivious or accustomed to it. Making no attempt to reach for a handkerchief he waits for his companion to recommence walking. As more of the worm oozes out, its lower end, the oily part that first escaped, wriggles down and across the man's chest. Neither he nor his companion acknowledges it. Indeed, even when the companion turns his back it is not a gesture of revulsion but merely preparatory to walking forward trailing the sack and the worm-ridden older man behind him. The worm begins a jerking motion as if trying to wrench itself out of the nostril.

'For God's sake!'

The cry is doubly alarming. Inexplicably, it is heard in a world previously locked in silence, nor is it uttered by either of the two men. Far more shocking is the immediate response to this appeal. A black, swift-moving shape sweeps down from the winter sky and brushes the worm away. In the instant it is perceived the shape vanishes again in the flat stratus. The worm has gone but no man can say whether it was carried up through the cloud or brushed into the open grave. The shape from the sky is surely the hand of God, yet the undertakers ignore it as they ignored both the presence and passing of the worm. Believable that they might not acknowledge the worm, familiar as they must be with the corruption of bodies, but to ignore God? Yet in the moment the hand of God was laid upon them they had merely recommenced walking toward the grave.

At the graveside the sack is dumped onto the ground. Again it deforms and sags. The repetition of this reaction, and at a graveside, confirms for the watchers the content of the sack. There is more than one body in it, and as only two bearers are needed, the bodies are not those of grown men. It contains the uncoffined bodies of children or dwarves.

The senior bearer begins punching his fists together, holding and striking the cold air. The younger man, young in his fifties, struggles along the edge of one of the earth mounds, his feet slipping in the claggy marl. He is afraid he may slide into the pit where the worm waits for him as it waits for all. The man turns to face his companion, bends again to the sack. Together, the two men half-drag, half-lift it over the edge of the grave. Then, with a callous gesture of relief they half-throw, half-drop it into the pit. The silence is not broken by the heavy fall of it.

In continuing silence the undertakers walk to the nearest yew tree, stoop, obtain shovels. They return to the grave and, with the same air of resentment that characterized their carrying of the sack, begin to fill in the pit. Soundlessly, the shovels bite the earth; soundlessly, earth falls onto the little corpses; soundlessly, the men spurt their breaths indignantly against the cold air. When the digging stops shovels are thrown back under the yew, muddied shoes are ineffectually dragged and toed in the frozen grass. The pit and its mounds now have the appearance of a normal size grave. There must be another body or bag of bodies to be interred. The undertakers walk off left taking the dawn with them. Momentarily, the watchers are in impenetrable darkness. Then the scene is re-illuminated and new confederacies of images appear.

Most garish is the vivid green grass that now decorates the dug soil, turning simple fact into grotesque parody. Of all those now assembled at the grave only the occupant of the coffin is unaware of the burial earth beneath the humpy plastic lawn. The people gathered include the two undertakers, now accompanied by four colleagues who gently lower the gleaming coffin into the grave, retrieve the black tapes, step away. The mourners shuffle slightly closer. The priest is speaking — but soundlessly.

The mourners are many and smart. The few women are fur-wrapped, men heavily buttoned up in expensive overcoats, hats held embarrassedly at thigh or in crook of arm. It is clear that great bureaucracies and corporations are represented here. Bland faces of blamelessness. Duty is being done, little grief felt. It is easy to identify the widow. That one truly grief-stricken face, above black furs, stands stark against the polite solemnity of her companions. Even the young man holding her arm, presumably her son, appears uncommitted to grief. He, like others, is here in performance of the expected gesture rather than in agony of loss.

The atmosphere of rehearsed charade is heightened for the watchers by the silence which neither priest nor respondents can fracture. The feeling that something is wrong is apparently communicated by the watchers to the widow. She turns her ravaged, bewildered face on the mourners seeking support, explanation. Some return her gaze, others look away.

As heads move, as collars are pushed awry, the watchers themselves become restive. They are recognizing mourners.

Now, the priest attempts intervention, mouthing words directly across the pit toward the widow. She, with a gesture that might be one of disgust, throws a single red rose down onto the coffin, down onto the wasted beauty of the wood. There are no other flowers. The son scatters earth disdainfully. The mourners disperse.

A large untidy man carrying a spade emerges from behind a yew and strides purposefully toward the grave. Not even his brutal task produces any sound. As he digs and fills, tiny unlovely snowflakes begin to fall on his back, onto the earth, onto the plastic grass now so carelessly tossed aside. As the gravedigger's spade slices deep he strikes a power line. The graveyard flares into a white light that consumes the gravedigger and blinds the watchers.

2

'Whose tatty film was that, sir?' I asked.

'The PM lent it to me,' said Frimmer, gnawing his cigar. 'And our tatty projectionist let his hairs crawl all over it.'

We were allowed a moment to speculate upon both the implied chumminess of the PM and the bollocking our projectionist was to receive. But there would soon be matters more important.

Frimmer's bunker was heavy with more than the weight of earth, steel and concrete that buried it. After the film show, he had ordered Wilson, Green, Douglas and me to join him there. Obediently, we had trailed out of the projection room and across the lawns. Waiting for the others to catch up with me, I had looked up to the burgeoning hanger woodlands on the Chiltern slopes, had drawn a deep, chilled breath, had known I was home again in England. Then the four of us had plunged down out of the weak spring sunshine into this underworld. Of course, Mr Stone was there too. As Frimmer's deputy he required no invitation. Now, pinned by silence and anticipation, I realised Mr Stone was smiling at me. He is probably a very nice man, kind to children and animals, but his smile is pure laxative. Obediently, my sphincter twitched. My companions seemed relaxed, anxiety-free even; but Mr Stone had not smiled at them.

Sitting to attention on my right was our grey mastiff: Detective Chief Inspector Arthur Wilson. On the other side of him, Detective Sergeant Jim Douglas stifled a yawn with one hand, elegantly manipulated his cigarette-holder with the other. He wished to be thought of as an elegant lounge lizard but nothing masked his basic crudeness, the vulgarity of that long horsy face. Beyond him sat the gorgeous Detective Inspector Susan Green. And she, as if to prevent my regarding even her as charming, was leaning over on her right buttock so she could scratch her left. Never can tell with those old cinema seats in the projection room.

The four of us, arranged in a broad arc, faced the great desk behind which Frimmer and Mr Stone sat on back-tilted chairs. What were they really thinking as they stared at us through the blue cancerous haze of cigar and cigarette smoke? Here, buried deeper than any grave, things were no more what they seemed than in that film. It had been appropriate to show us burials. We were all, in our time, images of death.

DCI Arthur Wilson sat to attention not because of ambition, but because he was still troubled by a back injury sustained in a car smash. The three men in the other car, armed bank robbers who had killed, had died when Wilson forced them off the road. It was rumoured our man had knocked a survivor back into the blazing wreck. Saved a trial. The fire chief had commented that car and corpses must have been burning for a long time before Wilson had radioed for assistance. But his back injury explained the delay well enough. DS Jim Douglas's most recent killing had been a simpler matter. As he was attempting to arrest two armed men they had decided the odds were reasonable. Only one had lived to limp round a prison yard on crutches.

And me: Detective Sergeant Jack Bull? I had ended the life of a sad, bereft woman against whom not enough could be proved. I had been her angel of death: no psychiatric gaol for her. Since then I had been to the USA where, in a bitter New York blizzard, I had left two Negroes and a Caucasian police lieutenant dead in an alleyway; their involvement in an international drug ring terminated. Their plan had been to leave me in the alley. But they hadn't known me very well.

If all this left Stone and Green with brighter images, he had only to raise the steel hook that replaced his right hand, and she the wig that hid her scars. They had had their share. And Frimmer? No one knows his past but it must have been gruesome if he's chief. Nothing about him ever suggested sweetness and light.

'Well?' barked Frimmer, jamming his cigar back in his teeth, letting the front legs of his chair slam down on the floor.

To my dismay my colleagues offered pronouncements on the film I had only a question. And when DCI Wilson made a remark about a mourner who represented the Prime Minister, I felt something a lot stronger than the pricking of thumbs. Apparently, a highly significant event had occurred while I had been working undercover in New York. Susan Green looked across at me and grinned. Annoyed that she had seen my bewilderment, I scowled at Frimmer. He decided on rescue.

'I wanted you to see the film because you are the members of the Serious Incident Unit to be involved. That was the funeral of Sir Gregory Fortis, one time supremo of British Intelligence services. In telling you the man's name and former occupation I am doubling the number of non-Intelligence personnel who know this.' He inclined his massive head, looked at the papers on the desk top, gave us time to assimilate the weight of this remark. The Prime Minister had not conveyed this information to the Cabinet. Taking advantage of our breathlessness, Frimmer spoke again. 'He died last January in somewhat bizarre circumstances. The Press got a D Notice and were only allowed to refer to untimely death of retired civil servant. A Dorsetshire coroner got a secret inquest without jury. His verdict was completely proper and in accordance with the evidence. However, our Intelligence colleagues carried out a very thorough undercover investigation of their own, but were satisfied their former chief died as a result of a tragic accident.' Frimmer paused again, sucked his cigar, waited for the question. DCI Wilson obliged.

'Why do they want SIU to see their film three months afterward?'

'*They* bloody don't,' said Frimmer, gleefully. 'It was the PM who insisted. Told 'em they'd had their chance, done their own checking and come up with roses. Time now for an independent investigation.'

'But what stirred things up again?' asked Wilson.

'Some clever bugger took a shot at the village bobby, a PC Bradford Ashmore. Happened three weeks ago, fourteenth

March,' said Frimmer.

'Poacher?' asked Jim Douglas, languidly. I suspected he was just as hooked as the rest of us.

Frimmer smiled at him. 'With an Armalite rifle?'

There was another silence. Smoke drifted. Someone sighed. That sort of gun was enough to guarantee our interest. In fact the gun was more important than the fate of the local woodentop. Charitably, Jim Douglas enquired.

'Missed him,' said Frimmer. 'Hit his handlebars. His good luck turned out to be ours as well, because as he and bike were knocked into the road he saw a piece of bark fly off a tree in the roadside wood. Gave a clue where the bullet might be. Forensic were able to find the tree where it finally came to rest. Dug it out, tested; opinion: Armalite.'

'Someone just happened to be around to work that out, sir?' said, DCI Wilson, sarcastically.

'No,' said Frimmer, acknowledging the point of the question. 'Intelligence really *had* pulled out. It was the local force, including the intended victim, PC Ashmore, who got the ball rolling. He knows enough to know what sporting guns sound like. He was also riled by the implication he hadn't got his patch sorted, never mind someone wanting him dead. Resourceful man by the sound of things; even got himself a new bicycle. Argued that fitting new handlebars wouldn't do. Claimed the whole bike was evidence and that he must not interfere with it by riding on it.'

'Like the sound of him,' whispered DCI Wilson.

I didn't. But then I didn't like the sound of any of it. For SIU to be sucked into a security matter meant trouble.

'So where do we stand, sir?' asked Jim Douglas.

'No problem,' lied Frimmer, expansively. 'Our intelligence colleagues had their chance. And now we have a directive straight from Number Ten. However, to avoid muddying the waters I'm putting in junior officers under cover. I've already informed Intelligence of this, and they've agreed to keep their hot little hands off the case, partly because of this quite specific directive from Number Ten. So if they do try anything you can hit them as hard as you like.'

I cursed under my breath, depressed not only by yet another lie from Frimmer but also by the feeling there was something fuzzy about the operation, something out of focus. I could imagine groping my way into a morass for something that would be painfully obvious once I'd identified it. Hindsight would make me look a fool. (God! If only I'd known!) I was keen enough to return to active service now I was back in England but not in a shambles like this.

'Right,' said Frimmer. 'We've prepared case files for each of you giving the background you need. You will each sign for your copy but may not take it out of this room. If you need to consult the papers again after today you will do so here and nowhere else. Issue the files please, Mr Stone.'

'Excuse me, sir?' I said.

'What is it, Bull? I'd rather take

17

questions after you've read the file.'

'Just one, sir,' I persisted. 'What was in that big sack?'

'Why, Bull, the bodies of Sir Gregory's killers.'

3

The night of Sunday, the 4th of January, was exceptionally cold, but dry and clear. The snow of the previous two days still lay cold-crusting on the ground. There was no moon. At 7.30 p.m. Sir Gregory Fortis, wrapped in his old Crombie overcoat, and also wearing a cap, boots and leather gloves, left his house by the back door. He intended to let the dogs out for the night. As a senior civil servant there was apparently no requirement for guard dogs for himself, but he had married money, and Lady Fortis, formerly Miss Isobel Artress, owned fine collections of paintings and jewellery. These she had acquired upon the death of her first husband, Max Stapolous.

The guard dogs, three Dobermanns, were released every night to run free on a strip of open ground between two concentric circles of fencing surrounding the house and gardens. Once the dogs had been released into this compound visitors could only reach the house after telephoning from the gate house a mile away and waiting for the dogs to be rounded up. Then electrically operated steel mesh gates were opened in both fences, the visitors drove through, the gates were shut and the dogs released again. Not surprisingly, the Fortis family had no casual callers at night, and invited guests usually stayed overnight.

Sir Gregory himself was in charge of the dogs. They responded to him as if they were overgrown puppies but would have torn anyone else to pieces. Neither Lady Isobel nor her son, Sir Gregory's stepson, Nicky, dared go near the creatures. The somewhat bizarre result of this was that the dogs were only released when Sir Gregory was at home. The guard dogs were available to guard Sir Gregory but not to guard the family treasures when he was away. The local inhabitants regarded this as an eccentric arrangement only to be expected of the rich. However, it was well known that a highly efficient electrical alarm system had also been installed.

On the night of the 4th of January Sir Gregory followed his usual routine. He let himself into the compound between the fences and locked the gate behind him. He walked the fifty yards from the gate to the fenced-off section of the compound where the kennels stood against the inner fence. The dogs were waiting for him and, as usual, set up the distinctive blood-chilling barking that announced Sir Gregory's approach. The noise was heard by Lady Fortis and Nicky as they sat before the great fire in the library drinking sherry. Dinner would be served at 8 p.m. after Sir Gregory returned from the kennels and had drunk his glass of sherry.

Sir Gregory unlocked the gate of the kennel enclosure and the three dogs immediately tore him to pieces. The thickness of his overcoat and gloves may have given him a moment's protection, but it was probably the case that one of the dogs leapt straight into his face. What remained of his corpse and the condition of that remnant rendered explanation a matter of guesswork.

The hideous noises made by man and dogs during that dreadful death reached the people in the house. Sir Gregory's stepson ran to the back door and, delaying only to find a torch, went out into the grounds. He stood at the inner fence and shone his torch into the compound. By this time only the dogs were uttering sounds. Nicky was violently sick and leaned against the fence. Immediately, one of the dogs raced across the intervening space and hurled itself at the wire. In his statement Nicky Stapolous said that only his own quick reaction saved him from being mauled through the wire mesh.

'The animal was spotted with my step-father's blood and obviously deranged by the taste of human flesh. I returned immediately to the house and, although I knew there was no hope for my stepfather, told Tomkins the butler, to phone for police and ambulance. I told the housekeeper to attend to Lady Fortis. I fetched a gun from the gunroom, returned to the compound and shot all three dogs. With the spare key which I had obtained from my stepfather's study, I unlocked the padlock and entered the compound. All the dogs were dead. I dragged their bodies away from my stepfather's body and back into the kennel enclosure. I covered them with a tarpaulin and locked the kennel enclosure gate. I was unable to touch my stepfather's body but threw my jacket over the top of the trunk where the face and neck had been. I went back to the house, joined Lady Fortis who was naturally extremely distressed, and together we waited for the police and ambulance to arrive.'

As an addendum to his statement Nicky Stapolous had summarized the action he took the next day.

'I called in our local vet, Mr Barnard Hardwicke, to examine the dead dogs. He found no obvious explanation for their complete change in behaviour. He agreed to carry out tests on samples taken from the dogs, but these tests failed to suggest why the dogs had attacked my stepfather. Mr Hardwicke has only been able to speculate that the extreme cold may have contributed to their condition. Mr Hardwicke is a widely respected authority on Dobermanns and a highly successful breeder of the species. It was from his kennels that my stepfather obtained the three dogs.'

I returned the copy of Nicky Stapolous's statement to the file. It was a very thin file. Apart from the police reports and the stepson's statement about the man's death, the only other document referring to Sir Gregory Fortis was a very brief summary of his Intelligence career. I suspected Frimmer had had to fight hard even for that.

Sir Gregory had been an exceptionally successful agent and field officer and, subsequently, a field controller for Intelligence. He had spent considerable periods of time both in Czechoslovakia and Poland. He had survived field operations to become an equally successful administrator. He had been several times promoted through ranks unspecified until, at age 54, he had been appointed by the Prime Minister of the day as overlord of all the Intelligence services. It was a post which at that time the general public did not know existed and the heads of the various M.I. services probably wished did not. Six months after appointment as Supremo, Gregory Fortis had been knighted. Just over eighteen months later, shortly after his fifty-sixth birthday, he had retired. I pushed the papers back into the file. A further two years on, age 58, he had died that terrible death only a few yards from the peace and safety of his home.

Waiting for Frimmer to return to the bunker I stared at the map-covered wall, wondering what the career summary had not mentioned. Had Fortis ever been betrayed, captured, turned, escaped? Had he been retired from the field only on age grounds? And why had he resigned that top job after only two years? I don't know much about conditions of service — secret or civil — but it seemed something of a waste of a good man. Nor was there reference to any link between resignation and a big change in his private life.

Eight years earlier, at age 50, he had

married Isobel Stapolous, née Artress. It was his first marriage. She was then 32, and her son, Nicky, was 12. Apparently, the marriage was successful, and they had been living in the same house, The Hall at Testem Magna, for the eight years of their marriage.

Perhaps he had retired from the paperwork, from reporting directly to an uncomprehending Prime Minister or Ministers. Was that it? Perhaps he resigned shortly after a general election gave him a new and unacceptable boss. I don't like the word perhaps.

'You people ready now?' asked Mr Stone. The four of us looked at each other, nodded. Mr Stone pressed a button on the big desk. Less than a minute later Frimmer walked into the bunker, gestured at us to remain seated, sat behind his desk.

'Well?' he said, lighting a fresh cigar.

'Not a lot,' said Arthur Wilson, quietly. We all nodded in agreement.

'It seems so straightforward, don't it?' said Frimmer. 'If it hadn't been for that shooting incident — well.'

'Did our Intelligence colleagues link the two incidents?' asked Arthur Wilson.

'If they did they ain't telling. They certainly did not raise the possibility with PC Ashmore for fear of compromising security. He knows nothing whatever about Sir Gregory's job.'

'So why do *we* assume a connection?' asked Susan Green.

'In one sense we don't,' said Frimmer. 'We're just interested in any case where someone tries to kill a copper with an Armalite. On the other hand *is* it only accident of geography that the shooting incident occurred in the village where Sir Gregory Fortis died?'

No one answered his question. We were all trying to get to grips with those two straightforward but possibly related incidents. Everyone involved appeared to have reacted appropriately and correctly. So what else might have been done? That gave me an idea, the true significance of which we all missed. (Later, I came to recognize that moment as the one where the groping began.)

'Yes, Bull?' said Frimmer.

'Well, sir, there is one other thing that might have been done. The only check on those dogs was carried out by the vet who supplied them in the first place.'

'Ah,' said Frimmer. 'Not so. Apparently, PC Ashmore foresaw the potential for trouble in that arrangement. He persuaded Mr Hardwicke, the local vet, to get a second opinion.'

'Did he?' said Jim Douglas. 'Enterprising little sod, is he? You thinking of recruiting him for SIU, sir?'

'Yes to all questions,' said Frimmer. 'Anyhow Mr Hardwicke was pretty stroppy about the idea, slur on his professional skills etc. But he came round when Ashmore stressed the advisability of protecting his reputation as a breeder. The other vet did postmortems and gave the dogs a clean bill. They had been in good health, had not been drugged or otherwise interfered with. Their stomachs were empty but that was not surprising. Sir Gregory had reared them to be fed only in the mornings; helped to ensure their enthusiasm for night-time guard duties. Both vets are positive there was nothing physiologically wrong with the dogs.'

'And who decided to bury them with their victim?' I asked.

'Probably agreed between widow and stepson. Stepson claimed responsibility perhaps partly to protect his mother from further questions. No evidence to suggest she objected. And it's not so strange when you think about it. Apparently, Sir Gregory had been genuinely fond of the dogs, and they had been his guard dogs for several years. Other questions?'

'Yes, sir,' said Susan Green. 'Sir Gregory didn't hold down that job for very long, did he?'

'No,' said Frimmer, curtly. 'And we've got no information on that. I've been told very firmly that matters of internal policy in our security network are not my business, nor are they relevant to the case. It was grudgingly pointed out that a different view might have been taken had Sir Gregory's death been anything other than an accident.'

'Was there an election just before he resigned?' I asked.

'No, Bull. See your mind's working on the same tracks as mine and Mr Stone's. No. I am being completely truthful when I say there is no known explanation of his sudden retirement. Of course, I am disbarred from quizzing the ex-Prime Minister on this subject, for the reason I referred to a moment ago: internal security matter, therefore not my business.

'Right. You all see how it is. There is no way in which the death of Sir Gregory can be murder. On the other hand the attempted murder of the village policeman cannot be dismissed. So, I decided to respond to the Prime Minister in the manner most beneficial to us in SIU. I've agreed that we will check every detail yet again, and we will also launch a field operation with myself in charge, and with Wilson as recording angel.

'Now, I'm not prepared to tie up my men and resources for very long in what is probably no more than a cosmetic exercise to improve our standing with the PM. Those of you put into the field will have to decide pretty damn quick if there's a case for us to follow up. If there isn't I'll pull you out and leave the shooting incident to the local force.

'Other questions? No? Right, this is how you're going to get in there!'

4

On Tuesday, the 5th of May, at 4 p.m.,
PC Bradford Ashmore was waiting for us
at the crossroads just north of the village.
He was leaning against the signpost, new
bicycle propped across his thighs. He was
in shirtsleeve order, helmet pushed back
from his forehead. No one else had
braved the heat. Susan Green brought the
Range Rover to a halt beside him. I stuck
my head out of the nearside window and
grinned.

'This the road to Testem Magna,
Officer?'

He looked at me blank-faced, then
jerked his head upward at the signboard
above him. 'Says so, don't it?'

'I may report you for cheek or for
resembling a photograph of PC Ashmore,
well known bicycling acrobat and live rifle
shooting target.'

'Thankee sir, I'm sure,' he said,
touching the edge of his helmet with two

fingers. 'And I recognize the registration number of your vehicle. You must be Dr Bull.' He leaned forward for a moment and stared directly at my driver. 'And the lovely Miss Green. Two well known archaeologists just returned from North America. Welcome to Testem. May your stay be extremely short but fruitful, leading to commendations for the village policeman.' He slumped back against the signpost.

'Possibly,' I said. 'How about meeting at the Steelstones tomorrow morning, 10.30?'

'Yes, sir. Meanwhile, get your good selves settled in at the Wheatsheaf, and spread the word about your interest in our local archaeological sites. Doubtless someone will gossip to me in the bar and I can then remark that I will be up to the site to see you're doin' no harm to the national heritage. Good luck, sir — and miss.'

'On yer bike,' I said. Susan let in the clutch.

As we drove away I watched him in the nearside wing mirror. He was still leaning there in the afternoon heat, blond hair poking out like straw from under his helmet, uniform shirt a smock on his tall spare frame. He looked much younger than his thirty-eight years. He was not looking in our direction but staring straight across the road at the far hedge.

'Some people have the life,' I said, half-amused, half-irritated. It was possible PC Ashmore was our only ally.

'You think so, Jack?' asked Susan, changing gear. 'The way he looked at me he obviously thinks you're the lucky one.'

'Well, you are very beautiful,' I said, almost crossly.

I still had not come to terms completely with Frimmer's plan that had put me and Susan Green into the field as archaeologist and assistant. I accepted he was not prepared to put in a man alone, not with gunmen lurking in the hedge-rows and intelligence agents in the drains. But why pair us together? And his coarse remarks about the areas in which I might assist her may have amused Jim Douglas and Arthur Wilson but they'd got deeply embedded in my right nostril.

Felt like that undertaker in the film.

However, my initial resistance had been undermined by several factors. The first had been Susan's own response to the plan. She had said she accepted it as the best way to work on the case and protect ourselves at the same time. The second factor was that I recognized she offered that response out of a far more extensive and more bloodstained experience than mine. Another factor undermining my resistance was rather different. It was lust. The prospect of getting my hands on, my leg over, etc. etc. (perhaps partly as punishment for previous rejections?) was so appealing to my animal self I also acceded to the plan. Don't learn, do I?

Our preoperational training had further modified my former resistance. I had spent twenty-eight days with my highly professional female colleague admiring her toughness and dedication. And, at the same time, there was constant reinforcement of lust: that superb body moving next to mine in the gym, on the assault course; her lovely face locked in concentration at the indoor range where I got the worst scores for months. 'Concentrate on the bloody target!' the instructor had snarled. (She had been afflicted by coughing at that point.) The instructor had gone into a corner and talked quietly to the wall.

But something more significant, more subtle, had also begun to affect our relationship. Her hard professional shell resembled an ill-fitting suit of armour. Through the gaps and joints I had glimpsed aspects of her real self: the softer, warmer, humorous woman under the metal sheath. I'm not denying my stoked-up lust, don't want to, but I had added other feelings, other dimensions to my perception of her. I could not say if those new feelings in any way related to love because I did not know any more what love was — or is.

In addition to all the extra physical and small-arms work that preceded every operation, we had also been required to rehearse our shared fictitious past. We needed to be word perfect for any social occasion where our relationship might be discussed. That had been a joint learning exercise in which we had questioned, checked and cross-checked each other about how we had first met at an archaeological dig, and how she had subsequently become my field assistant and secretary.

Our introduction to archaeology had also brought us together in a new way: in shared ignorance. A distinguished field archaeologist had been given two weeks to introduce us to the rudiments of practical and theoretical archaeology. He had done his best and so had we, but the results felt pretty shaky to all three of us.

Archaeology was a key to our operation in two respects. In the first place it justified our stay in Testem Magna, surrounded as it is by some of the most interesting archaeological sites in Wessex. Secondly, archaeology had been Sir Gregory's only hobby apart from his dogs. It had been a major factor in his decision to make his home in the area, and his interest in local sites was well known. Fortunately for us no other member of his household had shared his enthusiasm; so it was just possible that the superficiality of our knowledge might not be detected.

Despite these preparations, Susan and I remained unhappy about various aspects of our roles; not least the reversal of rank and status they involved. I was rather happier about that than she was — naturally. Our other two colleagues were also unhappy. DCI Arthur Wilson was responsible for the books. That he was still recovering from injuries prevented him from taking a field role but logic had not soothed. He had left us in no doubt our efforts were to be supervised by a hungry hawk. Detective Sergeant Jim Douglas was the other unhappy member of our quartet. His role as runner and back-up he regarded as degrading. When I had ventured the opinion I was very happy to have him watching my back he had made the coarsest of responses. I had replied in similar style. We had parted both amused and angry with each other.

'Nearly there,' said Susan, calling me into the present. 'You hear what I hear, Jack?'

'Motor bike?'

'Yes. Behind us. I'll slow down.' She put the gear in neutral, let us coast down a slight incline. From somewhere behind us, to the north, a motor bike was moving at about the same speed and in the same direction as ourselves. 'Do we stop before we reach the village?'

'No,' I said. 'Keep going. See what happens.' No need to remind each other that our guns were neatly packed in a case in the back of the car.

She let us roll until our speed was down to fifteen miles an hour, then she engaged gear, accelerated over the next few yards, then coasted again. The motor bike was gaining on us. Then we were in sight of the village.

Testem Magna is laid out in a plan that resembles a lower case letter e stood on its side. The bar of the letter is the north-south main street. The curves are the lines of houses overlooking the arcuate greens that have made the village famous. These broad curving greens mark the original position of a great circle of stones, a circle nearly two hundred yards in diameter. Only one huge stone remains upright. The others had either fallen or been completely removed. The men who had broken the stones and taken fragments up to the downs probably did so about two thousand years ago. Perhaps they had taken the magic of the site with them, and that explains how a village grew up here. Most stone circles in Britain have been avoided as settlement sites. The curved greens lie east and west of the main street and, with devastating originality, are named East and West Greens.

We halted in the main street outside the Wheatsheaf. The motor bike seemed even closer but perhaps that was because Susan had switched off our engine. The village lay silent under the early May sun. There was no one in sight but it was not a deserted village. Several net curtains had twitched as we arrived.

'Sounds as if he's turned off onto the track beside West Green,' said Susan. She was right. If he continued on that curved track he would come eventually to its junction with the main street through the village. We would see him then about eighty yards ahead and south of us.

Then he was there: helmeted and black-leathered despite the heat. He stopped at the road edge, looked both ways, crossed our road and continued onto East Green. Did he really look for longer toward us than in the other direction? He was riding through the Greens and round us in a huge circle.

'Cowboys and Indians?' said Susan, staring at me.

'Could be. Let's sit here a bit longer. See what he does.'

What he did was complete his ride round the village and rejoin the road we were on about a hundred yards behind and north of us. Then he turned north and accelerated away in the direction from which we had all come.

'Pity we packed the binoculars,' said Susan.

'Maybe. Probably had mud on his number plates.'

'Even in this drought,' she said.

We listened to the sound of his engine

dying against the downs overlooking the village.

'Been more bothered if he kept circling,' I said.

'Maybe,' said Susan. But we both knew a disposition of forces had been confirmed, that some other contact had been made in addition to that vital one with PC Ashmore. So we sat there and ruminated on the possibilities of a case to answer, of a well informed opposition to face; an opposition aggressive enough or frightened enough to try and murder PC Ashmore.

'Hot in here,' Susan complained. 'Let's find mine host. We're on time.'

I stepped down onto the pavement and slammed the door. I watched her walk round the front of the car to join me: wig gleaming in the sun light, the flowing of her body encased in white sweater and the short denim skirt that had excited PC Ashmore. And that slightly mischievous curve to her mouth. All the heat and tension of the afternoon were suddenly caught in my throat. Damn and blast bloody Frimmer! Did it have to be this way? One day, one golden day it wouldn't be. I grabbed her left hand, led her up to the door of the little hotel. The only sound she made was the soft clatter of her sandals as she hurriedly fell into step beside me.

5

The Wheatsheaf, being on the left side of the main street, had East Green behind it and there, almost in the hotel garden, stood the only surviving complete and upright stone. It stood only thirty yards from the window of the room into which the landlord showed us.

'You'm taken by our stone then, Dr Bull?' he said, plump face creasing up. 'Everyone gets taken by that when they first come in here.'

'I'm an archaeologist,' I said, curtly.

'Oh, well, you'll be even more interested then, won't you, sir. You know its name?'

'The stone?'

'Ah. The Testing Stone it's called. Yerse. No one knows why. But that's always been its name as long as folks hereabouts can remember. Now, miss, about breakfast tomorrow, Wednesday morning?'

I could understand why he'd turned to

talk with Susan. Somehow the stone had possessed me. Partly its size. Nearly twenty feet high, eight feet broad and with sharply angular corners, the great sand-brown cuboid stood facing me. I was troubled by the idea it might as easily represent something of the future as of the past. Mentally shaking myself I checked that it really was thirty yards away and would not strike the wall of my room if it fell. But something about it negated distance. The stone seemed to be an extension of the hotel, of my room, of my own body. Far away, in Samarkand, I heard Susan and the landlord talking. Something was said about me that provoked kindly laughter but I did not turn, did not speak.

Staring at the stone I began to appreciate the complexity of its surface forms; it was not at all a simple cuboid. Surfaces were marked by undulations and depressions that suggested a beast tensed and hunched. At the vital moment of springing forward it had been magically locked up in stone. When release comes the beast will be ready poised to spring forward. I knew exactly where the foreclaws would strike.

I stepped backward, blundered into our landlord. Startled, I apologized. He made some cheery dismissive comment and left us alone together with the stone.

'Our Mr Wentall's very talkative, Jack.'

'Mr Wentall?'

'The landlord, Jack. You all right?'

'Yes of course.'

'Nice room you have.' I nodded. I supposed it was. It was dominated by a double bed that resembled a miniature Testing Stone lying on its side. Susan turned her eyes full on me. For a moment they were flecked with a colour deeper than grey. Perhaps it was light reflected from the blue-grey bed cover. 'We have to decide, don't we?'

'About?' I said, brutally.

'Don't be bloody. About our relationship.'

'So how do you want to play it?'

'No, Jack. It's not a question of wanting. It's what works best.'

I felt my heart slide downward from my rib-cage and into my loins. Her words struck deeper than was appropriate merely as denial of lust. I looked out of the window again. 'That stone is tremendous, isn't it?' I said.

'Yes. I suppose it is.' Behind that non-committal response I suddenly recognized pain. She, like me, experienced the demands of our work as denial of feelings. I turned to face her, and we saw ourselves mirrored in each other's expressions. She recovered first, stood up, came and put both arms round me. Astonished, I replied in the same way.

'We both know what we're doing,' she said. 'If we become lovers, however casually, it will affect our work, maybe cost us our lives. Remember how poorly you were shooting on the indoor range? And all I was doing was standing there. I know I can read that as a compliment — and indeed I do. But how would I feel if somewhere else you missed a target and died?'

After a long time we moved apart a little. I kissed her gently between the eyes. 'Susie!' I said. We let go of each other.

'Better get the rest of the cases, Jack.'

While getting the other cases from the car I had time to check again the empty street; time also to curse my imagination. To do the latter was stupid of me; imagination is one of the gifts for which I am hired. SIU specializes in difficult cases: cold scents, no-hopers, dead ends from ordinary police work. As a result there is a significant place in what we do for imagination and intuition. My problem was that imagination was getting out of control. On the other hand, I told myself defensively, as I hauled two cases up the stairs, there *were* some interesting hooks for imagination.

What did PC Ashmore feel while standing out in the sunlight at the crossroads? He had survived one attempt on his life but perhaps he was still a target. Not so surprising he watched hedgerows rather than the back of our vehicle. And who had taken the trouble to ride a motor bike into the village at precisely the time of our arrival? And as for the Testing Stone — well! The sheer weight of history and mystery it carried was sufficient hook for imaginings. I blundered into Susie's room with her cases, put them down beside the neat little single bed that nestled against the dividing wall. Another hook for my imagination. *And* the stone could also be seen from her window.

I went back to my room and discovered Susie was unpacking the guns. (That motor-cyclist had got to her as well; or perhaps it was the defencelessness of a policeman standing at a crossroads.) She sat on my bed with the small black attaché case open next to her. Light glinted on the spare shells in the case. Our two pistols lay on the leather on her lap. Then she picked up her pistol and began to check it. As she ejected the gleaming shells I stood and watched. Even as I watched that scene — the cool, shadowed bedroom, her blonde hair falling over her cheeks as she bent forward intent on her task, pistol held in front of the voluptuous swell of her breast — I knew it would never leave me. I felt it being etched into the surface of glassy memory.

'All right?' I asked weakly.

'As ever,' she said. 'No problems with our armourers. Always the perfect job. Are we carrying?'

'Not yet,' I said, absurdly pleased to be asked. After all she was senior in rank and years: one rank and four years. 'We don't even know what we're up against yet so let's stay in role. We can lock the whole lot away, then put that case inside this one and lock it as well. We've no reason to suspect we're blown. One inquisitive motor-cyclist don't indicate a breakdown of security.' There was a knock on the door. 'Wait!' I said.

Susie put both guns into the case, shut it, carelessly put it on the floor beside her. She took a pen and small notebook out of her bag.

'Come in,' I said.

'Sorry to disturb you, sir,' said Mr Wentall, his eyes sweeping the room, taking in the luggage, the case of books open on the floor, Susie's pen and notebook held ready. 'Thought you'd like a pot of tea, sir.'

'Thank you,' I said, taking the tray from him, barring his way.

'Er — right, sir. Dinner at eight o'clock but the bar opens at six.'

'Thank you,' I said again. He shut the door and walked heavily along the corridor. 'Safe enough?' I asked.

'Better safe than sorry,' she said quietly.

'Right. You pour while I get out the shaver.'

I put the battery operated shaver on top of the dressing table and switched it on. Very slowly, like a perambulating black slug on a choice plant, it began to rotate. After two complete revolutions I switched it off. 'All clear,' I said, and heard her sigh. We both knew the ridiculous mistake we had made: to come into a strange room and start talking before checking. Frimmer would go mad if he ever found out. No use for us to say it was his fault for pairing us together so intimately.

'Thank goodness,' she said. 'Have some tea. We obviously need waking up.'

When tea was over and Susie had gone to her own room I felt depressed. It was a combination of sadness about our decision, and that peculiar sense of partial

51

disappointment, part regret, that possesses the traveller on arrival at his hotel. The room was so ordinary with its standard furniture and furnishings, mass-produced prints ostentatiously framed: a determination not to be homely. I was reminded of a remark by an international art smuggler whose job obliged him to use many of the world's great hotels. 'Never be surprised if people act out of character in a hotel. It's partly a reaction against the anonymity, the professional disregarding by the staff. Being hand-cuffed to you is positively friendly.'

Moving very slowly, I unpacked my case; not cheered by the noises from Susie's room suggesting she was doing the same thing. At the bottom of my case was a new notebook and my old pens. Maybe there would be time to write my way out of despondency and into new poems. Our cover as field archaeologists suggested free evenings. I put the pad and pens on the small table that stood next to the bed and in front of the window. I looked out at the Testing Stone. It, and all its fellows in the circle up on the downs, were of a sandstone found only in Devon. The huge blocks had been dragged many miles from the west. The west. I remembered that the Ancient Egyptians believed that where the sun sank was the land and place of the dead.

6

Two hours later Susie and I met in the bar. She looked marvellous in a silver-blonde wig, black blouse, long red skirt, black shoes. I was absurdly relieved I had chosen to wear a suit. Three drinks later, and seated at a corner table in the dining-room, I found it difficult to return her glowing look. It was as if recognition of what we had agreed to deny was now a stimulant; maybe denial implies promises for the future. I pretended to complain about the way she looked at me and she pretended to be sorry. Then we were laughing together like children. How could I tell her then that she was my unicorn; that she had the power to turn my sorrows to joy, my pain to growth? And how was it that I, psychic smart-alec, never considered that she already *knew* the power she held for me?

We were served a good meal, drank a bottle of wine and just floated. Part of my mind was trying to tell me I had not felt like this since just before my fiancée had been killed, but I shut it all away, drowned myself in the moment. Later, having a nightcap in the bar, the real world — the other real world — was not so easily excluded.

'What would you like?' rumbled Mrs Wentall, smiling fatly out of arms akimbo. As I gave our order conversations that had almost stuttered to a halt at our entry picked up again. In one corner a London accent was sawing wood while softer country tones mused together over the chippings. That voice was a parody of a voice we knew; the Scottish lilt had been deliberately planned away to leave a more strident version of Jim Douglas. Susie winked at me over the top of her glass.

We sat on a settle in the corner furthest from Jim and enjoyed the performance. We gathered that as a highly successful salesman — 'into double glazing' — he was taking a holiday. Business being a bit slack in May he was indulging his favourite hobby of photography. He was not actually staying in Testem Magna but touring the area looking at villages and churches.

'Reelly based on Salisbury,' said Jim. 'But I branch out 'ere and there, follow up what I read in guide books, the local papers, usual sort of thing. Can I get anybody another?'

The Wessex voices were suddenly clear and incisive. Jim emerged from his corner with a tray of empty glasses. Not looking in our direction, he tottered to the bar, towered over Mrs Wentall. She was glad to see him bearing so many empties. Jim made much of the exercise of checking her arithmetic, and then offered her a drink which she somewhat stiffly declined. Back in his corner he was soon allowed to re-establish vocal control while his four companions purposefully sipped their ale. If one of them bought the Londoner a drink every time he bought them four . . . And listening was cheap.

'Yes,' said Jim. 'Local papers 're a lot of help in finding interestin' places. Don't mind just driving about of course, but saves a bit on the old mileage if there's a particular destination.' Something was muttered at him. 'Oh no, not always in double glazing. Sold all sorts. Used to be in dog foods. Mind you, I hear you've got a funny way of feeding dogs round here.' Jim gave a coarse guffaw. There was a moment of appalled silence as his remark hit everyone in the bar. But Jim sawed on, apparently oblivious he was cutting against the grain. 'Heard about it only yesterday when I was on the way here. Something about an old boy being chewed up by his own dogs, wasn't it?'

Someone in Jim's corner gruffly agreed with this. Then the softly spoken phrases: accident, bad business, not local but a good man, joined in the life of the village.

'Strange kinda accident,' said Jim, beerily. 'Never heard of one like that before. Reckon someone must've been tormenting the poor buggers. What were they?' A soft voice uttered the name. 'Christ,' yelped Jim, 'Wouldn't fancy me chances with them. Where'd'e get 'em from?' Again a soft answer. 'Local, eh? Thanks for the tip, friend. I'll be careful about trespassing with my camera. Pardon? No, sorry to say no, but won't have another. Must be on the road. What? No, like I said, I'm not staying here tonight but might be later in the week. I'm booked in in Salisbury till Thursday but I might move over this way after that. Depends. I know you chaps are fed up with the drought but it makes good picture-taking weather everywhere for me. Don't much matter where I am. Well, goodnight gents. Enjoyed talking with you. Might see you later in the week.'

He stumbled from the corner, bade Mrs Wentall an ornate good evening and left the bar. As the door closed behind him sly laughter drifted from the corner where his drinking companions sat. 'Know him when we see him,' someone said. As if to emphasize his credentials Jim over-revved his car, stalled, restarted. Laughter rose louder in the bar.

'Setting himself up well,' whispered Susie.

'Yes. Even a hint he might move in here. Now I think *we* do a little selling. I'll get more drinks.'

'Mr Wentall tells me you're an archae-ologist, Dr Bull,' said his plump spouse, drawing my pint.

'We both are,' I said, loudly. I could almost feel furry little ears cocked behind me. 'We've come here to do some work up at the Steelstones and over at the Ring.'

'Dare say,' she said, slightly aggressive. 'There was a time when people came to see the Testem Stones and Greens. We seem to be out of fashion these days.'

'Not at all,' I said, warmly. 'This place is world famous. It's just that archaeologists did a great deal of work here before the Second World War. So we know your Stones and Greens pretty well.'

'World famous, are we?' asked Mrs Wentall, appeased. 'Nice to know that.' Obviously, she considered herself to be speaking for the whole bar, the whole village.

'Oh, yes,' I said. 'When my assistant and I were working in America earlier this year I think we were asked just as many questions about Testem Magna as about Stonehenge. And we will certainly be taking another look at this site even though it's not included in our work programme.'

'You been here before then, sir?'

'Years ago as a student,' I said. 'But this is my colleague's first visit.'

'Ah. And you say they asked about us in America? Didn't know they 'ad much archaeology over there.' Mrs Wentall folded her arms, America disposed of.

'Well nothing as famous as Testem Magna or the Steelstones, but they have quite a lot of Indian sites. We have just been working on an Indian site in Georgia. Very interesting.'

'And how long might you be working with our places?' asked Mrs Wentall.

'We'll be here for at least a week but we have permission to work on the sites for longer if necessary.'

'Well, Dr Bull, don't you be surprised if Brad turns up when you're working.'

'Brad?'

'Oh yes, sir. PC Brad Ashmore. He's very hot on vandalism is our policeman.' She was quite unaware she had just offered an archaeologist the ultimate insult. I decided to stay nice.

'You had a local resident interested in archaeology, Sir Gregory Fortis.' We both

60

enjoyed the moment of silence, of glasses half-raised to mouths. 'I had hoped to meet him during this visit but then I was notifed of his death.'

'Oh yes, sir. Dreadful business that was. They kept it all quiet at first, you know. But these things get out. Tragic accident it was. Killed by his own dogs, you know.'

'Really? That's horrible. I'd heard he was dead but nothing of the details. Rather makes me wish I hadn't written to his widow confirming our meeting.'

'You goin' ter see Lady Fortis?' Mrs Wentall's voice rose an octave. I could not decide if the lounge bar was more stunned by her squawk or my remark.

'Well — yes. When she answered my letter she invited me for tomorrow, Wednesday the Sixth of May. Is there something else wrong that I don't know about?'

Momentarily, Mrs Wentall was unable to reply. She seemed to be wriggling her stout body into a more comfortable relationship with heavily boned underwear.

'No, nothing *wrong*,' she gasped, slumping more comfortably against the bar. 'No. It's just that since the funeral there's hardly been a visitor allowed — except some rather strange folk down from London. But no one local allowed in. And they've changed all their staff as well; got new people in from a London agency, so they say.'

'Strange folk?'

'Well, perhaps not strange. But they've been havin' some pretty wild parties up there recently. The son's been running things very different to his father, his stepfather that was, I mean.'

'You think they should still be in mourning?' I asked. The unexpectedness of my question, and the interpretation of events it implied, had a remarkable effect on Mrs Wentall. She lost her voice. As she stood before me opening and closing her mouth I knew my identity was established in the village, perhaps even more firmly than Jim's. I was the man who had taken Mrs Wentall's breath away.

'Dunno,' she said, sullenly. 'Suppose that might be it.' She gave me the look a stupid woman reserves for a more stupid man.

'Might be?'

'Well she, Lady Fortis, never seemed that close to her husband. He was her second, you know, and much older than her as well. Count on the fingers of one hand the times in eight years you'd see them about our village *together*. Course, he was like you, interested in stones and things, and I suppose she weren't. But I wouldn't have said they was close, if you see what I mean.' I did but didn't speak. She had something else to tell me. 'And there's been a lot of them parties since. Friends down from London, like I said. But maybe they're friends of the son. They do say his mother can't do much with him.'

'So you think I'm lucky to have been invited up to the house?'

'Suppose not, really. After all you're a stranger here yourself. P'r'aps she's decided it's all right because you're *not* local. What time will you be going up to The Hall tomorrow, sir?'

'Afternoon. I'll be back here in good time for dinner. My reason for going is to see some papers in the library. I understand Sir Gregory was preparing notes for a paper on the Steelstones, and as it's unpublished I want to see that original copy.' Mrs Wentall opened her mouth but I spoke first. 'We're pretty tired after our journey today. Would you mind if we took our drinks upstairs?'

'Er — no, sir. That's quite all right.' Anything else she might have said had to wait because someone else came to the bar to order. I escaped.

As Susie and I left the room carrying our drinks, conversations began to swell in every corner. No doubt part of the talk would be speculation about the duties of an archaeologist's lady assistant. No doubt they would get it wrong, I was sorry to think. As I followed her upstairs I acknowledged that the Wheatsheaf had potential as an information centre. News of new arrivals would soon spread whether they came by car or motor cycle.

7

At 10 a.m., Wednesday morning, Susie and I were standing speechless in the centre of the Steelstones, looking out between them toward Testem Magna in the valley below. Somewhere above us, beyond the soft gold of the haze, a May sky flamed over Wessex.

The village, and the hills that curved up on all sides like folds in a woolly blanket, trembled in the morning light. The soft colours of rooftops, of flat-topped hills, of small hanger woods, pulsed gently in the heat: buildings and rooves from brick red to rust brown, almost to orange; green downlands from yellow-green to emerald. Here and there isolated buildings made of local stone vanished in the haze and reappeared apparently in quite different locations. Somehow, Susie and I were equally insubstantial. Only the stone circle stood firm, holding us on the hill.

The Steelstones are unique. Although

the stones stand in a very large circle, about the same diameter as the Aubrey Holes at Stonehenge, the stones are much smaller and there are no menhirs as at Stonehenge. In some respects they resemble the Rollright Stones. They rarely exceed four metres in height and are crumblingly pyramidal in shape. It is the angularity and jaggedness of these stones which has been cited to support the theory they are broken remnants of the great stones that formerly stood in the village below — marking out the great circle now represented by East and West Greens. This theory is further supported by the fact that they are of the same pale sandstone as the Testing Stone; that one solitary, sinister survivor still standing in the village. That the stones had been moved up to the hill summit is also considered by some archaeologists to be evidence for a change in function. Their original religious significance in the valley had been replaced by an astronomical and mathematical function on their newer hill site. Why the Testing Stone was left behind no one knows. It had already occurred to me that perhaps it had survived in its original position merely because our ancestors had failed to break it down into smaller more easily transported pieces.

Whilst thinking of all this, and of Susie's right thigh now contacting my left, I realized the light was changing, the mist lifting and dispersing in the sunlight. The gauzed sun now became visible as a rinsed pale yellow disc, deceptively small, cool and distant through the thinning haze. The sun's emergence darkened and sharpened the shadows thrown toward us by the Steelstones on the south side of the circle. Dark with light: analogy for a love affair. Susie broke the spell.

'Why the Steelstones?'

'Very prosaic explanation,' I said. 'A local name reflecting their suitability as sharpening stones. It's reckoned that every house within ten miles has a chunk chipped off these stones and kept in a kitchen drawer. The locals swear by it; supposed to be far more effective than any back doorstep or stone window-sill.'

'So they're still useful,' said Susie, with satisfaction.

'Yes. And I think we need to look as though we are. Better unpack some gear from the Range Rover.'

We walked a south-easterly radius of the Steelstones, passed between two of them and out into the open downland. Ahead, discreetly located in a small fold of the downs, was the car park. As we stumbled toward it, I think we both wanted to believe that no one else would ever come to that place. That dream went the way of all dreams — but brutally. As we came over the rise any pleasure we might have felt, because our car was still the only one in the car park, was negated by the darkly dressed figure leaning against the bonnet. As Susie and I walked down the slope together, but with yards between us, PC Ashmore leaned unmoving against the front of the car and stared at us. When we were only three strides away he spoke but did not move.

'Morning, Dr Bull, ma'am.'

'Morning,' I said. Susie said nothing.

'Nice day,' said PC Ashmore, stolidly.

'Yes,' I said. 'Unusually hot for end of first week in May. We're just going to set up shop and get some surveying equipment out.'

'Very wise, Dr Bull.'

'I'm not really a Ph.D., you know.'

'No matter, sir,' said PC Ashmore, still unmoving. 'It suffices. And since I have been told you are both senior to me, superior even, it contents me to call you sir and ma'am — appropriately of course.' Relieved by the faint glimmer of humour in his last remark I asked how we should address him. But the shutters had come down again. 'PC Ashmore is appropriate for matters of business, sir. Doubtless you will discover that my fellow-yokels refer to me as Brad behind my back. But only thus to my face if trying to hide something. Most have learned not to be misled by my friendly face and apparent youthfulness.'

'Not on duty today?' I asked, staring at his dark suit.

'Unofficially, sir. Village constable does not really get a day off in the manner of big city policemen. I am alone here. Old man Humphry just as likely to beat his woman today as on any other. And that

Fred Seaton does not restrict his poaching to the days I'm helmeted.'

'And does your day off prevent you helping us up the hill with our gear, Brad?' asked Susie.

'Not at all, ma'am. Especially as I'm supposedly here to ensure you do not sharpen your pencils on the Steelstones nor carve your lover's heart in the rock.' She gave him a hard glance but no glimmer of mischief marked his face.

As we laboured up the hill with the surveying equipment, feeling the heat beginning to stir in the ground, seeing the mist clear completely from the hilltops, I considered the possible causes of PC Ashmore's reserve. It was not merely a matter of senior officers being several years younger than he (I was 28, Susie 32), nor was it his resentment that he knew so little of what was going on. It was *both* these facts together and combined with realization he had to continue as a target for as long as it suited *us*. A lot of anger there.

By the time we had put down our loads just outside the Steelstones I had decided my approach. I suggested we all sit down. Before he did so, PC Ashmore carefully removed and folded his jacket revealing a snow-white shirt set off by his dark tie. He sat on the ground between us and slowly rolled up his shirt sleeves. Beside his neatness I felt myself a cowboy in my check shirt, faded jeans and sandals. Despite the heat he did not loosen his tie. He sat there with a certain primness I found irritating.

'So what did you do wrong?' I asked him.

'Dunno, sir.' He very deliberately ran his right hand through the corn thatch of his hair. 'I think about it a lot. Had two months to do so, haven't I? I've gone over every call I made, every place I passed. Nothing.'

'But someone wanted you dead,' I said, harshly.

'Yes, sir. And still does?' The infuriating man said no more but stared steadily out over the drought-locked downs.

'How about your arrests, court cases round about that time?' asked Susie.

'No, ma'am. A few fines in the local

court — licence offences, that sort of thing. Touch of domestic violence, a young tearaway sent to Borstal. Nothing more.'

'Had you been up to The Hall?' asked Susie. This seemed a dangerously revealing question but I bit on my lip, reminded myself I was junior help.

'No, ma'am, no need. Sir Gregory's death was all cleared up several weeks before I got shot at. I believe the son to be something of a hothead but he gives no trouble. A few wild parties up at The Hall, but that's all kept within the estate. Not even a problem with a drunken guest driving through our lanes.'

PC Ashmore continued to look across the summer land as if nothing had changed, but Susie's question could never be retracted and he was no fool. His keen ear must have picked up the neutral tone of his questioner, just as his eye must have examined the faces of the mourners down from London for the funeral. The speedy arrangement and discreetness of the inquest, held in a distant part of Dorset, would also have been noted. That may have been the moment for taking him into our confidence but Susie remained silent. So I took his mind elsewhere.

'Your private life?' I asked. The calm way he accepted the question, dwelt upon it, caused me to admire the infuriating man even more.

'No, sir,' he said, eventually. 'Happily married, Debbie and me — except we can't have children. Brothers, sisters, parents, all get on with us and with each other. In the family manner, you know? A few arguments, occasional row, but nothing that leads me to think — well, think that.' He paused as if reconsidering. 'Other factor is what I've been told about the shot: solid shot from a high-powered rifle. No such gun around here. No call for it. A few two-two's, shotguns, those kinds. Nothing else.'

'Have you been told anything else about the incident?' I asked.

'No I have not!' At last the calm manner cracked. 'I have been frequently reassured by my superiors that my safety is of great concern to them, and that investigations continue. My role is to keep my eyes open on my patch. Should I now feel safer because my local cover has been withdrawn and you are now my guardians?'

Neither of us answered the question. We sensed he had already guessed that we represented a potential for trouble far exceeding anything he had ever known.

'Yesterday afternoon,' I said, changing tack again, 'when we saw you at the signpost north of the village — '

'Yes, sir?' He was calmer.

'Did you stay there for long?'

'That I did. Several minutes. A fairly public place, sir. One is less likely to be shot at a crossroads.' The anger stirred like a snake under his words.

'Did a motor-cyclist pass you leaving the village?'

'No, sir. Important, sir?'

So I told him about the motor bike, the coincidence of it being ridden through the Greens just as we reached the village.

'That so?' he said, rubbing his hands over his face. 'It seems you'll not tell me why this matters, but I'll tell *you* another

74

thing. That rider didn't pass me going in behind you either.'

'And there are no side turnings off that road between where we left you and the village itself,' said Susie.

'Correct, ma'am,' he said. 'So cross-country seems to be the manner of his coming and going.'

'You heard him?' I asked.

'Probably,' he said, suddenly rising to his feet. 'I was listening for many things.' He picked up his jacket. 'I bid you good morning and ask you not to deface the stones.' I thought of the sounds he had been listening for during the last eight weeks. Which are the sounds that suggest a safety catch eased off, a rifle cautiously raised in a hedgerow, a finger taking up first pressure on a trigger?

I watched him walk down the hillside. The convexity of the land first hid his legs, then his body, finally the blond crown of his head. He looked like a man walking bravely down into his grave.

8

At 2.30 p.m. that Wednesday afternoon I slouched against a stone wall shaded by dry oaks and stared at the main gateway to The Hall. The twelve foot high wrought-iron gates stood wide open. On top of one gatepost a unicorn stood poised in prance. I looked at the other post, expecting a lion, but saw a second unicorn facing the first. Both wore conspiratorial expressions. All three of us knew what unicorns do.

On the other side of the drive, and also shaded by trees, stood a small gatehouse. Behind the front garden wall a skinny, bright-eyed, grey-haired woman prodded the vegetable patch like a missel-thrush breaking snails. I wondered where she found the energy in that heat. Between us the tarmac of the drive lay like a trail of lava. I would soon have to walk on it. The old woman kept one eye on me as she gardened but I wasn't quite ready to make trouble. I was enjoying the shade while listening to the engine note of the Range Rover fading away as Susie drove toward Salisbury to make phone calls and meet Jim Douglas.

The letter I had received that morning, confirming my meeting with Lady Fortis, instructed me to report at the lodge before making my way down the drive. Being a good detective I had decided to ignore instructions given and make the most of a chance to look around. The lady thrush bent down behind the wall to wrestle an exceptionally resistant weed. I pushed off from my wall, raced through the gates and out of her line of sight. I heard her call out but I hid behind a clump of rhododendrons. She made no attempt to follow but went back into the house. I walked back, climbed the low wall of the garden, stood close to the open window. She was speaking somewhat sulkily into the telephone. A reprimand had been received.

'Sorry, sir, but 'e was too quick for me. Yes, I think it is that Dr Bull. 'E was dressed as you said. Right, sir. Sorry, sir.'

By the time she came out of the house I was fifty yards away down the drive. 'Dressed as you said.' That sort of information seemed to me, a mere townee, to go beyond the limits of ordinary village gossip. Not for the first time I wondered if some kind of conspiracy might be established against us. Only half-humorously, I wondered what it might be like to arrest a whole village.

As I followed the curve of the tree-lined, shrub-edged drive, designed so that The Hall could not be seen from the road, the lodge slid out of view behind me. The next bend would bring me in sight of The Hall. I stopped and listened. The world was clamped tight in heat. Then I walked on, rounded the second bend and stopped again; this time as if stuck in melting tarmac. There were no more oak trees or rhododendrons. The drive stretched ahead Roman-straight but without a single tree to mark its course. The scattering of discoloured wood shavings, the pale stumps protruding through the grass like patches of human skin, indicated the recency of the fellings. The maps and photographs in Frimmer's bunker were more out of date than we had suspected. The drive now stood bald above the surrounding fields, the margin marked only by a new, disfiguring post and wire fence.

'Field of fire,' I said, stupidly addressing the last in the line of surviving oaks on my left. But I recognized that no one could approach The Hall via the main drive without being in the open for at least fifteen hundred yards. And I was unarmed. Not that a pistol would be of the slightest practical use over fifteen hundred yards, but it would have been a comforter, my little piece of blanket. Then someone else offered a more adult comment. From the direction of The Hall came the sound of a motor bike engine. Relieved that I had not yet committed myself to the open drive, I plunged behind the last of the surviving rhododendron bushes.

At fifteen hundred yards a motor cyclist is not even identifiable; at one thousand yards he begins to be so; at five hundred yards you realize just how fast he is coming at you. I crouched low. A hundred yards before he reached me he throttled back, changed down for the bend. Helmeted, black-leathered, he swept past, accelerated, then checked for the second curve that would bring him to the lodge. I scrambled up the slight rise and back onto the drive and began to walk briskly toward The Hall.

The clear afternoon light brutally emphasized my feelings of exposure on that road raised like a causeway above the surrounding fields and hedgerows. I knew I was not going to make it across the open ground. So, when I heard the motor bike revving up, when the black ant began to rush after me, enlarging its size and my fear as it tore along the drive, I just stopped walking and turned round.

He drove straight at me, braking violently at the last moment, stopping with his front wheel at my kneecaps. He raised his visor but I didn't hit him. I recognised him from the photographs: Nicky Stapolous, Sir Gregory's stepson, stared at me haughtily.

'Dr Bull?'

'Nicky Fortis?' I asked, spitefully.

'No. Stapolous. Would not permit my stepfather to adopt *me*. But where the hell were you, Dr Bull? My lodge keeper told me you had started to walk. I should have passed you just now!'

'You were going too fast to see me,' I said. His brown face darkened still further. I was struck both by the rapidity of this response and the intensity of his rage. No need for him to speak to make me feel it. 'You offering me a lift, sonny?'

This kept him speechless. While allowing him a moment to recover I thought about his need to put on all his gear on such a hot day and for a round trip of two miles on his own driveway. Then he was able to speak.

'The prospect does not alarm you, Dr Bull?'

'You appear to have passed your test. Take me to your mother.'

'You could walk — sir.'

'No,' I said, cocking a leg over in the appropriate and offensive manner. The sensations of mounting behind him, of grasping at his slender, womanish waist under the cool slimy black leather, of pulling my body against his, were reptilian. Fanciful? Maybe so. But that response to Nicky Stapolous proved to be my one consistent response in all the short time I knew him. Then there was no time to ponder. He meant to impress.

He opened the throttle wide. The front wheel left the ground and we plunged up and forward in a mad rush of burning rubber and wasted fuel. I was obliged to hold him very tight; sweaty palms sliding on leather. He raced through the gears and The Hall began to rush at us. By the time we had cleared the first quarter mile the pull of acceleration had faded into a continuous buffeting of air. At half a mile, looking left, my head pressed behind his helmeted neck, I realized that the oaks were not the only feature that had gone from the landscape. The steel mesh gates that used to seal off the dog run across the drive had also vanished; so had the two concentric circles of wire fencing that had bounded the run. A quick look right as well as left confirmed that the whole strip of ground had been ploughed and then reseeded. A fresh green ring of lawn passed completely round The Hall. As we raced across that belt of land, little more than a cricket pitch in width, I realised that Lady Fortis and her son had constructed a model of the Greens at Testem Magna: a green circle cutting through the landscape. In the centre was The Hall squatting on its mound. I wondered what image would be offered as counterpart to the Testing Stone.

My driver made no attempt to brake as we approached the point where the tarmac drive swung left toward the rear of the house. I braced myself against him as he continued straight ahead and up the gravelled slope that led to the front of the house. With a spectacular showering of pebbles we slid and swung to a halt at the foot of the enormous flight of steps that led up from the gardens to The Hall. I suspected my driver was enjoying breaking some unwritten rule about bringing his bike here. The steps were to our left. Immediately to our right lay a large circular stone-edged pond in which a fountain played in a single slim jet and to a height of about thirty feet. Beyond, a broad walk led to lawns, flower-beds, green avenues.

Without speaking, the black figure of my mentor began to lead the way up the steps, removing his helmet and gloves as he climbed. He waited for me on the terrace at the top. Possibly, he wished me to admire the front of The Hall which appeared to be a miniature of Castle Howard. Perversely, I turned my back, looked out over the gardens below: some twenty landscaped acres set in lovely countryside. No wonder Sir Gregory had chosen to retire here. I brought my eyes from the view toward distant Salisbury and focused on the fountain at the foot of the steps. It played so cheerfully, with such cooling sweetness; how was it I saw it as the answer to my unspoken question? It was the polarity for the Testing Stone: fountain and rock; water and earth.

For the first time, I suspected that I shared with PC Ashmore those deep feelings of unease that arise from images speaking, however indistinctly, of more trouble to come.

9

The cool entrance hall was an echoing white cliché of high, domed roof, slender pillars, double flight of marble stairs, and every wall hung with sombre, undistinguished oil paintings in heavy crenellated gilt frames. Here, Nicky Stapolous disdainfully handed me over to a small dark gorilla. It had the same stocky build as myself but was about six inches shorter, and had rocks where I had muscles. It had a complexion like the underside of an old frying-pan. I assumed it to be male. Unfurling a fist, he indicated I was to follow him. He threw open the library doors and, in a voice almost too deep for human hearing, grunted something at the room. I edged past him. He shut the door behind me leaving me alone. I sat on the edge of an upright chair.

Despite the presence of real books and not dummies, I knew I was on a stage set:

upper middle class English withdrawing-room, books optional extras; setting for late 1930's urbane, half-witted or witted Coward type comedy of manners. No one had ever felt affection for the room despite the quality of its furnishings and the acreage of carpet. I recognized the link between room and hall: a tasteless expenditure of too much money. Sir Gregory had married money but had spent it in that peculiarly graceless manner of the English upper middle class. I was allowed about one minute for feeling uncomfortable before Lady Isobel Fortis made her entrance.

Her dark, angular face, black hair, deep-set brown eyes, I had expected from the photographs, but her slenderness surprised. Moving like a dancer, she walked across Persia toward me, the soft folds of her red dress emphasizing rather than concealing her boyish figure. She wore no make-up, nor did I detect any perfume as we shook hands and exchanged greetings. I looked directly into her eyes as she spoke, was troubled by the intensity of her stare. That look conflicted with the coolness of her fingers in my palm, the youthfulness of her clear bell-like voice. Something watchful and calculating resided in her. And behind those barricades lay a shrieking anxiety that I would not be allowed to touch; something far darker than being widowed by dogs. We sat awkwardly, half-facing along the length of a huge sofa. She folded her hands in her lap, waited for me to begin. It was difficult to believe she had a son of any age, never mind twenty year old Nicky.

As I explained the purpose of my visit and expressed condolences on her loss, she looked down at her hands in her lap. The black pony-tail of long hair fell softly to the right of her head. The little girl thing was coming over very powerfully, yet I was consoling her on her second widowhood. As I spoke the empty formal words like a blessing over her bowed head, I registered another signal: brittle-ness. Her calm was not serenity but something held tightly under control. She was defence, anxiety and brittleness. I heard my words dying away against the glass-fronted bookcases of that shady grotesque room. I wondered what it was she was doing to me.

When Susie asked me how I found Lady Isobel I would truthfully reply: captivating. I would be speaking literally and as male. There was no doubting Lady Isobel's sexuality. But, for her, love would be about snaring, captivity and power; ball-crushing victory over a man. Perhaps it was *not* so remarkable she had been widowed twice.

'Sir Gregory was probably our most distinguished amateur archaeologist,' I said. 'The two monographs he produced were excellent. And, of course, he was also well known for his many letters and for his contributions at conferences.'

'Thank you, Dr Bull,' she said, unfolding and refolding her fingers in her lap. I noticed her fingers were exceptionally long in comparison with the whole hand. 'I received several letters of condolence expressing similar views.'

'I hope you found some consolation in them, Lady Fortis.'

'No,' she said, curtly. 'Letters are no substitute for a living person.' I stared at her. Something ugly was approaching the surface of our polite conversation in that stagy room.

'I understand Sir Gregory was also a very distinguished civil servant,' I said, almost breathless.

'Very.' The hands were still now. I wondered what it was she was not going to tell me. Perhaps much of her power lay in withholding, in negatives. At that moment I realized that some of the feelings of distress and distancing lay within myself. Fascinated though I was I was also experiencing her as repellent.

'Well,' I said, after a long pause, 'I hope the request for my colleague and me to study Sir Gregory's unpublished papers caused you no distress, Lady Fortis.'

'No,' she said. Another long pause. Perhaps she was still on some kind of tranquillizer originally prescribed when her husband died. 'Those papers aren't here.' Even as I allowed an expression of concern to crease my face, I detected a glint of something like amusement on hers. 'No,' she said. 'His papers are in his study upstairs.'

'Oh,' I said, playing along. 'For a moment I thought you meant they weren't here in The Hall.'

The malicious, silly little pinprick of her remark reminded me of the way her son had stopped his bike at my knees. Then, at last, she smiled at me. I did not fall off the settee onto my back with all four paws in the air.

'You may use the study,' she said. 'I'll get Nicky to show you the way. He'll be here as soon as he's changed out of his leathers. I hope he did not frighten you with that machine of his.'

'Not at all,' I lied. 'And it was certainly a relief not to have to walk all that way in the heat. My colleague has the car this afternoon.'

These words fell unacknowledged into a very deep well. So we sat in silence and waited for Nicky. Her manner appeared grotesquely inappropriate for a hostess rumoured to give wild parties. (Suddenly, I had an image of Susie sitting in a cafe with Jim Douglas in Salisbury. Would she, with that soft loving centre I had detected, be a match for this steel blade of a woman? I realized it was important for the two women to meet.) Then the door was flung open and Nicky came in.

He was wearing a white shirt, grey flannels and Gucci boots. The shirt set off his fine Greek face and brown skin to perfection. But I immediately sensed the scowl beneath the skin. 'Dr Bull ready?' he asked.

'Yes, thank you,' I said, smoothly. I watched his face. Young Nicky Stapolous was habitually and permanently angry. As I stood up so did his mother. Perhaps she was troubled that I had noticed her son's anger. She walked across the great carpet to where he was standing by the door, slipped her arm round his waist. As they stood next to each other and facing me, the power I had sensed in her became grosser, more overt. Their separate powers more than doubled when combined. Synergy is the word for that but the word I got was siblings. The fractionally taller younger brother stared almost challengingly at me; the shorter older sister looked toward me blank-faced.

As I walked toward them they parted, touched hands; then Nicky was opening the door for me.

'Thank you, Lady Fortis,' I said, staring directly into her face. Her dark eyes stared levelly into mine. I knew that at first meeting she already had some intimation of the disaster I represented. Then I was out of the room and ascending the marble stairs behind Nicky. At the first turn I looked down into the hall but she had not come out of the library to observe our progress. I wondered why that bothered me.

I discovered one of my several mistakes as soon as I entered the study. The charm and restraint of its décor defined the former occupant as a man of sensitivity and taste. I had been wrong to attribute the vulgarities of the library and hall to Sir Gregory. Someone else was the vulgarian. The only link between library and study was absence of any family or individual photographs.

'Charming room,' I said.

Nicky Stapolous grunted. He was standing in the doorway watching me. I

92

walked to the bookcases that lined one wall. 'Good collection,' I said. No response except the deepening of his frown. I walked crabwise before the books, reading names aloud. He continued to glare at me. So I slipped in a couple of fictitious names just to check him out. 'Atkinson, Behrend, Clayton, Coles, Fairman, Grinsell, Harding, Hawkins, Hawkes, Lockyer, Piggott, Thom, Williams, Wood.' No response. Then opportunity for a direct question. At the end of the bookshelves one unit of shelving was filled with box files labelled alphabetically. 'What's in those?'

'Eh — offprints. He got photocopies of many research papers of the last few years.'

'You helped your father?'

'My stepfather. No! Could not see the interest. The old — my stepfather — tried to drag me into it but he wasted his time.' Nicky's immobility was suddenly disturbed by abrupt folding of arms.

'So what will happen to all these papers?'

'Not a surprise to me if she asked you

to take them all away for your university. Mean nothing to us, I assure you.'

Yes, I thought. Smoothed away, wiped out like that strip of new grass round the house.

'Is that a possibility?' I asked, falsifying enthusiasm.

'Er — well — not for me to say. You must ask Lady Fortis.' Anger was griping him again. 'I suppose you want to stay here? Not more than an hour, please. We are busy preparing for a party tonight.'

'Can my colleague and I return here later in the week?'

'I will have to check with Lady Fortis.' He flounced away leaving the door open: I walked across the room and closed it.

Undisturbed, I spent half an hour browsing in the study, trying to understand Sir Gregory by looking at the manner in which he had lived his great passion. Despite the hasty and elementary nature of my introduction to archaeology, I was able to recognize Sir Gregory's commitment and high level of scholarship. The carefully filed papers were also annotated in his hand, some of them at length. His map chest contained numerous field drawings of his own as well as copies of other workers' maps. His work had been of high enough standard to blur academic distinctions that might be drawn between professional and amateur.

My time spent in the study also helped correct or prevent another mistake. If we *were* working on a murder case we were in danger of neglecting the victim and what he still had to tell us. We were beginning to hear the voices of his place: his village, his house; we needed to hear him as well. His study told me he was not only a man of sensibility, education and enthusiasm, he was also a perfectionist. This latter conclusion I based not only on my sensing of a man striving for recognition in a field which others might describe as 'merely' his hobby, but also on the impeccable state of all the paperwork he had accumulated. Even his most hurried and brief marginal notes were neatly printed, accurately dated and linked to the card index system he had devised.

I may not know much about archaeologists but, for two reasons, I happen to know quite a lot about perfectionists. The first reason is that several of the more cunning criminals I had met in my work were perfectionists. That was sometimes their undoing. Secondly, I had for some years been trying not to be a perfectionist myself. So I know the two questions to ask. What is a perfectionist afraid of? And for what is the perfectionism a substitute? These two questions may be linked by their answers. For example, the perfectionist model-maker who may express his creativity in railway engines rather than in the feared sexual relationship of his marriage.

But things were not that simple: archaeology instead of marital passion. That might be true but there was also the disturbing factor of Sir Gregory's work. His job had required such attention to detail, such meticulous planning, as to satiate the mind and spirit of almost any perfectionist. But apparently this was not the case with Sir Gregory. So was there some deep-rooted dissatisfaction with his job, something to do with his decision to resign after so short a time in office? I stared out of the window, not seeing the new lawn, the fields. For the second time since that film show I experienced the sensation of being close to something significant but which was not yet identified. I know a bit about *that* as well. If I can't grasp a thing leave it just out of reach. Eventually, either it or I move closer. So I left it.

I also left the study and attempted a tour of the house. But I was frustrated by the number of staff preparing the house for the party. I wandered downstairs, followed a corridor stacked with chairs, small folding tables and cases of drink, until I emerged onto a courtyard at the back of the house. One side of the courtyard was open to the country, so I stood and admired the view. I realized I was standing at or close to the point where Sir Gregory had come out of the house for the last time on the night of the 4th of January. The place where the kennels had stood inside the fenced compound was immediately in front of me. Now there was no sign of it, no way of identifying its site. That circular belt of grassland passed blandly across the view. It was natural enough that the widow and son wanted to erase the kennel from the landscape, so why did I get exactly the same feeling as when I was in the study: the feeling of not quite seeing, not quite understanding? I was not allowed time to think about it.

'Lost?' Nicky Stapolous and the gorilla stood in a doorway next to the one by which I had left the house.

'No,' I said. The gorilla ambled across the cobblestones and stood next to me, very close. He smelt a bit like a gorilla.

'James can give you a lift,' said Nicky. James! A gorilla named James? 'He's driving the van into the village now to collect some more drink for the party. He's calling at the Wheatsheaf so he will take you all the way.'

'Thank you,' I said. 'I'd like to come back to work on your father's papers later in the week.'

'Any time,' said Nicky, surprisingly. 'Bring your colleague next time.'

'Should I check with your mother?'

'Lady Fortis has already discussed the matter with me.'

'Thank you,' I said.

'Upg pff khl,' said the gorilla. So I got into the blue van parked in the corner of the courtyard. I was not acknowledging the instruction so much as the possibility the gorilla had offered the only honest remark of the afternoon.

10

'So Frimmer wants to know if we have a murder case,' said Susie, pouring my second cup of tea. She was sitting on the bed in my room at the Wheatsheaf. 'Unfortunately, what you've just told me about Sir Gregory's house and family is extraordinarily vague; interesting but vague.'

'Yes,' I said, unhelpfully. 'Trouble is, Susie, there's something about *her* I haven't homed onto yet. Groping for words. It feels that she is far more deeply wounded, deeply damaged than can be explained by that bereavement.'

'We're all whistling in the dark, especially Frimmer,' she said, waspishly. 'We don't even have a reason to believe there was a murder. However gruesome Sir Gregory's death, gruesomeness does not turn an accident into murder. Nor does someone shooting at the local copper when no connection can be shown.'

'No, ma'am,' I said. She made a growling noise. Behind the play-acting she was acknowledging that my reputation for cussedness might be merited. 'So tell me your news, Susie. I've told you mine.'

'When I got through it was Frimmer who answered the phone. Decidedly tetchy because I had so little to report. Obviously, he is afraid this business could become a very expensive way to curry favour with the PM. Then he handed me over to DCI Wilson and *he* wasn't much better. I was left with the impression they'll be recalling us if nothing moves by next weekend. Wilson suspects we're getting a week's holiday at the taxpayer's expense.'

'They want blood, Susie. It's Wednesday today, so that leaves us about forty-eight hours to start something moving in a situation where nothing has moved since a possibly unrelated shooting incident eight weeks ago.'

'Ah, well,' she said, grinning wickedly. 'I haven't told you all my other news yet. First thing: there is now another guest staying here at the Wheatsheaf.'

'So?'

'Male, late thirties. Height about five feet ten, slim build, sandy hair, grey eyes. No obvious distinguishing marks. Wearing a light-grey suit, white shirt, grey tie, black shoes. Brown fibre suitcase bearing no labels. Name in the register is Henry Smith, London address. He arrived here about 4 p.m., driving a two-year-old pale blue Ford. He's in room six, two along from me.'

'Intelligence?' I asked. 'And at that age an experienced field agent?'

'Looks like it. Never learn, do they? Send 'em in looking so nondescript it's like uniform. They're as easy to pick out as CIA.'

'So what do we do?'

'I guess we take him out, Jack. I'll check with Frimmer but I'm sure he'll want him nicely packaged for presentation to the PM.'

'Dog with a bone,' I said.

'I also saw Jim Douglas as arranged. He's suffering acutely from boredom. But I told him to move in here tomorrow.

That cheered him up. He'll be even happier when he knows he can cut out Mr Smith.'

'Bloody Euston Station it'll be.'

'Maybe so, Jack, but my last bit of news suggests I did the right thing. I'd only been back here a couple of minutes when there was a phone call for us.'

'Here?'

'Yes. Mr Wentall came and fetched me. I'm still wondering if he recognized the voice when PC Ashmore asked for me.'

'Christ Almighty! What did *he* want?'

'A meeting this evening, 7.30 at the Steelstones. He thinks he's onto something.'

'Damn and blast it! Our cover could be blown by a call like that. What a bloody fool thing to do!'

'Not necessarily. How else can he contact us? He can't keep checking we're not chipping bits off the local stone circles. He also picked a good time, didn't he? We can still be seen in the dining-room by 9 p.m. We could say we'd been for a walk or that we had to drive up to the Steelstones because we'd left a piece of equipment behind. And locals and tourists are not likely to be up there at that time. As for Ashmore's cover, Mr Wentall told me the call was from the University of Cambridge.'

'But Ashmore's voice?'

'Ashmore told me he had disguised it until he knew it was me on the phone.'

'But did *you* recognize his voice?'

'Took you long enough to get to *that* question, Jack. That's the rub. I think I did, but on the other hand it could've been someone else with a local accent.'

'Christ! So what do we do about the meet?'

'Just in case it wasn't Ashmore on the phone we go separately and armed. Right, put this tea-tray outside the door so old man Wentall doesn't need to come in. If that woman at the lodge recognized you by what you were wearing I suspect mine host or his missus is a big mouth. Lock the door, then we can get out the guns.'

At 7.20 p.m. I parked our Range Rover in the Steelstones car park. I had dropped Susie off about half a mile back and not argued about it. If we were being set up we were both targets. I walked slowly up the hill, feeling the weight of my pistol against my left thigh. No shoulder holster. How could an archaeologist explain *that* away? A long pocket might at least seem suitable for carrying some small piece of archaeological field kit.

It was a lovely May evening, still very warm, but I neither removed the jacket of my dark suit nor stopped to admire the effects of the light and the long shadows across the landscape. I moved steadily up the slope, listening for any sound other than the soft swishing of parched grass against my shoes. As I climbed higher the tops of the tallest Steelstones were suddenly visible, creamy orange-white against the darkening sky. Higher still and I could see most of the nearest stones. Then, revealed in the final yards of the climb, like some passionate throbbing chord of music, the setting sun was poised immediately behind the stones. The great orange magenta sphere totally possessed the world at evening. The archetypal image of life, of the hero.

Feeling extremely unheroic I slipped

into the circle, stood with my back against the nearest stone. Apparently, nothing moved. Yet in that moment I experienced the polar feeling that everything *did* move; that the planet under the Steel-stones, under my feet, was turning us away from the glowing face of the sun at a speed my senses could detect. I was almost suffocated by that place at that moment; truly a place of revelations. Placing a hand against the stone I watched my fingers vanish into the rock as that weirdly beautiful light consumed them.

Voices slowed the spinning earth, grounded me in the familiar sense. Moving fast, I changed my position to the shadow side of a stone some thirty yards away. I drew my pistol, crouched low. The voices were closer, louder. Then Susie and PC Ashmore came up to the crest of the hill. Their voices died away as they too were confronted by the sun. I let them enjoy it, using their silence to check for other sounds. Nothing. I had intended to move slowly round the great circle but Susie's voice cut through the evening to reassure me.

'All right, Jack. It *was* PC Ashmore on the phone.' This was said without looking round. Ashmore peered in my direction but did not see me. I was stone. Then, very quietly, I moved toward them.

'I hope this is important,' I said, when five yards away. I suspect Ashmore's feet actually left the ground. Serves you right, I thought.

'It is, sir,' said Ashmore, watching me put the pistol away. Nor did it escape his attention that Susie and I were wearing dark clothes. 'My Super warned me that you people had a way of making things happen. I believe it wise to warn you of a possibility you have done that already. And this seems a suitable place to meet, sir.'

'As any,' I said, curtly, standing next to Susie and facing him.

'Tell me, sir, did you and your lady colleague really come down here to investigate my shooting?' I looked quickly at Susie who nodded.

'Ah, I see *that* now,' said Ashmore, smiling. 'I've been wondering who was

107

the senior of you two.'

'The answer to your question,' I said, sharply, 'is: yes, we did. At the same time there's a considerable interest in the coincidence of the attempt on your life coming so soon after the death of Sir Gregory, even though the latter was an accident.'

'I see,' said Ashmore, thoughtfully. 'I had begun to wonder if our Sir Gregory was merely a civil servant.'

'A rather special one,' said Susie, taking the plunge.

'I'll not embarrass further by asking details, ma'am. So to business if you please.' Behind his left shoulder the bottom of the rim of the sun burned a notch in the horizon.

'Go on,' said Susie.

'Well, ma'am. You started me thinking with your question about me going up to The Hall. You see, you are the only person ever to imply a connection between the attempt on my life and what happened at The Hall. Gave me something to think on, if you follow me?'

'Yes,' said Susie.

'I went back to my notebook, read through all the calls I made in the ten days before I was shot at. That is, the period forth to thirteenth March inclusive. *Now* the connection is apparent. On the eighth of March I called upon our local vet, Mr Barnard Hardwicke, with a query about a licence matter. I remember he looked very strained, even more so than usual. He is what I would call a nervous type. It is my belief that his life with animals is partly a substitute for an unsatisfactory life with people. But that's as it maybe. Because of your question this morning I have now recollected that my joviality on that occasion included some remark about how few of his favourite Dobermanns were in the big cages. I also recollected his very nervous response: something muttered about demand being less than previously.' Ashmore paused while I wrestled with the sensation that the sinking sun was rushing toward us emitting a deep, intense humming noise.

'So?' I said, almost deafened by realization.

'Correct me if I am wrong, sir,' he said.

(Correct him? I wanted to strangle the slow bugger!) 'But your concern for my welfare would take a very subsidiary place in your inquiries if the death of Sir Gregory was not an accident?' I nodded, speechless. 'Not my murder but Sir Gregory's is the real reason for your coming?'

'Murder?' said Susie, softly.

'Yes, ma'am. Only a theory, mind you, based on the idea you've put in my head with that question of yours.'

'For Christ's sake!' I snarled, raising a fist in the face of the sun now turning blood red. '*How* can it be murder?'

'They changed the dogs.'

11

'Your health!' I said, quietly, raising my glass at the Testing Stone. It continued to peer at me round the corner of the Wheatsheaf. I was sitting in the side garden at a bench beneath an old and very gnarled apple tree. I had the garden to myself except for a couple of farmers sitting at another table on the far side of the lawn. Had it not been for them I would have sat on that side where I could not see the Testing Stone, but I was expecting Susie to join me for a drink before lunch and she would need to talk.

As I waited our Mr Smith drove up in his pale blue Ford. It was the second time I had seen him since breakfast. He was pretty good at his job but I'm even better at mine. His fate would soon make him aware of that distinction. I felt no compassion for him, but would have preferred humiliation to be inflicted upon his idiot chief who mistakenly believed he could outflank SIU. Mr Smith parked his car on the other side of the low hedge that separated street and garden. Then he went into the hotel by the front door. As if representing weatherman and wife, Susie emerged from the side door at the same moment. She was wearing a crisp blue and white striped shirtwaister and white shoes, and carrying a white handbag and a very large gin and tonic in which the ice clinked cheerfully against the glass. She sat down facing me across the table, kicked off her shoes, scrunched her toes in the warm grass, raised her glass to me. I drank a little more beer. Neither of us spoke for a moment, our moment.

'Glad you found a table with some shade,' she said. 'It seems even hotter today.'

'How did you get on in Salisbury this time?' I asked, thickly. Had she *any* idea what she was doing to me?

'Everything set. Frimmer has now designated our operation a Murder Inquiry. SIU is rolling. I've brought back the radios for us. Jim's carrying his own.'

'And what time will Jim turn up here?'

'Just after lunch.'

'And Mr Smith?'

'As we agreed. We take him out this afternoon.'

'We?'

'Well, you and Jim. Frimmer's OK'd it. In fact he's looking forward to it.'

'Understandable. What an opportunity for him! We deliver an Intelligence officer neatly parcelled so that Frimmer can go along to the PM and say: 'Look what we've caught — and after they had promised you not to get in our way'.'

'And the justification for us, not that we need one, is that we don't want the field cluttered with strange bods; not at this sensitive stage,' said Susie.

'You're really going for Ashmore's theory, aren't you?'

'Why not, Jack? It's all we've got and it *could* fit the facts. Frimmer likes it and I like it.'

'Well, I won't argue — not until there's something specific to say. As for our Mr Smith, he obediently trotted after me this morning when I went up to the

Steelstones. I did a few sketches while he mingled with the tourists.'

'Let's hope you stimulated his curiosity. You'll mention going to Swallows Wood?'

'As we walk past him. He'll know well enough that's next to where Ashmore was shot at. How about our PC? How'd he get on in Acton Westhurst?'

'OK. He phoned through to me in Salisbury at 10.30 a.m. as we had arranged last night. He showed the undertaker photos of Dobermanns, and he said they were the type of dog he had agreed to put in the grave. Bit hoity-toity about it; not quite right for a respectable undertaker to be asked to do that. Couldn't quite refuse.'

'Wanted the business?' I said.

'Something like that. He said the dogs had been cut up by the vet's autopsy but he could still recognize them as Dobermanns. Ashmore pressed him on that point because the gunshot wounds must also have done a lot of damage. But the undertaker said that was not so, and that he was quite convinced that the dogs were of the same type as in the photos.'

'That's the rub: only the same type. Perhaps we need an exhumation order, Susie.'

'For what purpose? There are only two people who could distinguish between those three Dobermanns and another three — reliably anyway.'

'True enough. One's dead and the other did the swap.' I drank a little more beer. 'And the second vet's no use. All he could say in court is that the three dogs he cut up were the three put in the grave. He has no way of identifying them as being Sir Gregory's original guard dogs.' Despite the logic of my last remark I had the feeling there was something to be said for exhumation of the dogs. But no need to press. It wasn't as if they were going to run away or bite anyone.

'You seem a little less than enthusiastic about all this, Jack.'

'No, it isn't that. I'm willing to buy Ashmore's theory.' I looked away from her bright eyes. 'I think I've discovered the wisdom of not letting married policemen and policewomen work together.'

'We made our decision, Jack. Let's not exhume that sleeping dog either.'

I finished my drink. 'And what about the vet, Barnard Hardwicke? Is that set up as well?' I asked.

'Yes. Ashmore will call and frighten him this afternoon. He's invented some tale that justifies asking Hardwicke about sales and licences for Dobermanns in the last few months.'

'Good. And what about you, Susie?'

'I phoned The Hall and it's OK for me to go up and work in the study all afternoon. It was her ladyship I spoke with so maybe I'll meet her today.'

'Everything's set, good. But getting organized emphasizes the crucial question behind Ashmore's theory.'

'If they changed the dogs, who are *they*? Well, Jack, I still go for the view Hardwicke could easily have acted alone and for motives of his own.'

'And you think the main motive was sex?'

'Possible. It's clear Lady Fortis made a big impression on you. How might she affect a lonely middle-aged vet who comes up to the house to talk about animals with the husband? He is perhaps the one person in the village who could dream up such a murder. He is certainly the one person who could put it into action.'

'You think perhaps he went up to the house that day and switched the dogs all by himself?'

'Again — possible. He'd been up to The Hall several times so he'd've had a chance to get kennel keys copied. Don't forget that although the idea terrifies us, Hardwicke may have considered it part of a day's work. Maybe he also knew the family would be away that day. It's not something I want checked immediately but it gives us another frightener question to use after Ashmore's shaken him up this afternoon.'

'I rather hope that young sod, Nicky, wasn't away on the fourteenth of March. I'd quite like him to be involved in that shooting as well as the shooting of the dogs.'

'You've a malicious streak in you.'

'Could I be a copper without?' I said, irritatingly.

117

'You'll not get me caught up in that worn out discussion,' she said. 'Let's go in for lunch early so we can be on the start line by 2 p.m.'

As we walked out of the glare of the Testing Stone and the sun and into the cool dining room, I said loudly: 'So if you check those details in The Hall library I'll go down to Swallows Wood about 2 p.m.'

'Yes, Dr Bull,' she said, leaning lightly into me as we edged past the back of Mr Smith's chair. 'I'll leave about 2 p.m. as well.'

We did not glance in Mr Smith's direction. We knew his face would be expressionless. He was so good at being expressionless someone would eventually conclude he was sick. As for my face — it probably bore a thoughtful look. Interesting that in our discussion neither Susie nor I had suggested Lady Fortis might have been directly involved in the death of her husband. She had appeared to be genuinely grief-stricken in the film sequence of the funeral but since then I had met her, had sensed the depth of both her power and her anxiety. And what was working in Nicky Stapolous? Odd that he had not referred to Lady Fortis as mother but was so particular about stressing the correct relationship between himself and Sir Gregory Fortis.

12

Thursday's child on Thursday, the 7th of May, at 2.30 p.m., I stood in the clammy green heart of Swallows Wood. Like an insect sucked down into a human lung I felt the trees evapo-transpirating round me, against me. And I could hear Mr Henry Smith trying to climb quietly the boundary wall. I walked forward as noisily as possible, stopped again after twenty yards, listened. Welcome to Swallows Wood Woodcraft Folk, Mr Smith — but you're going to lose all your badges. Then I let my breath out, lifted my arm, wiped my forehead with the sleeve of my conspicuous white shirt. Apart from unicorns grazing no other creatures moved; no birds sang.

I spent a few minutes pretending to examine a large sarsen stone. The trees in that part of the wood had grown too close together for the stone to have been carried between them. Not that that proved anything about the placement of the stone. The life expectancy of trees is as a day in the sight of great stones. Hysterical Bull? But the biblical turn of phrase led naturally to the next: where one or two are gathered together . . . I had picked up the discreet sounds of Jim Douglas entering the wood far away to my right. Our last radio contact, more than ten minutes ago when the unfortunate Mr Smith was out of my view, had confirmed Jim's sighting of both of us and his intention to move in from the right.

Walking very slowly, I continued toward the lane on the far side of the wood; the lane where PC Ashmore had been shot. I walked, Mr Smith followed. I was towing him across Jim's line of approach. I strolled across a small undulating clearing, stopped at the far side. To avoid discovery (As he thought!) Mr Smith would have to stop before entering the clearing. I stood and waited. Later, I thought Mr Smith sighed very softly but I did not turn round.

'OK,' said Jim Douglas. Then I turned. Jim was leaning against an ivy-smothered tree, a bundle of old clothes at his feet. As I walked toward him he bent down and rearranged the clothes to resemble Mr Smith. Brutally, he dragged the body by its legs away from the edge of the clearing and back into the trees. At the base of a young oak tree, with his victim lying face down, he arranged the legs on each side of the tree trunk, then bent the body up and back against the tree so that Mr Smith was in a kneeling position. Before he could topple forward Jim pulled the arms back and round the tree, handcuffed the wrists together. It looked an extremely painful posture and, as Mr Smith came round, found himself on his knees, hands cuffed behind the tree, he began to moan quietly. He was soon to discover that being unable to protect the front of his body was more painful than the hand-cuffing. He looked up at the two of us; slightly longer at Jim whom he had not seen before. Then his head dropped and he muttered something. Almost casually, Jim leaned forward, slapped him hard across the face. 'Stop complaining,' said Jim.

Mr Smith fell silent. Not even having his pockets picked by Jim caused him to speak.

'Well, well, Mr Henry Smith,' said Jim, roughly stuffing Mr Smith's possessions back into his pockets, 'You appear to be a blameless gent.'

'What's this about?' asked Mr Smith, trying to sound unruffled.

Without warning, Jim struck him a second, more vicious blow across the face. Mr Smith's nose began to bleed. Apprehensively, I looked at Jim. I had not seen him at work before. Jim winked at me but it was a humourless gesture.

'Now, Henry, my dear,' said Jim, taking out a pocket-knife, flicking the blade open under Mr Smith's nose, 'we can, as they say, do this the easy way or the hard way.'

He bent lower and, with one smooth flowing stroke, slashed open Mr Smith's trousers parallel to the zip. Mr Smith had just enough time to flinch, to realize that Jim's knife must be very sharp, before the point was stabbing at his genitals. Mr Smith tried to move backward, his knees pushing frantically in the leaf mould.

Then his spine jolted against the tree. His face began to turn grey.

'Now, now!' said Jim. 'No unpleasantness will occur provided you answer a few questions. I'm not going to ask you what your people could regard as top secret, just for local field information. So feel free to talk, mate. The other reason for talking is obvious.' Jim's hand moved quickly and Mr Smith expelled all the breath from his lungs. I must have made some kind of sound as well. Jim scowled at me. 'Take a walk. Ten minutes,' he said.

Shamefacedly, I walked away in the direction of Longbottom Lane where PC Ashmore had nearly died. In this part of the wood some of the larger trees were leaning sideways. The disturbance under their roots had occurred recently and none of the tree trunks had developed a curve back to the vertical. The ground was moving under them and under me. The further I walked the more undulating the surface was and, in the depressions in the ground, the vegetation had a dark lush quality I had not seen anywhere else in the locality. And there was a stench of woodrot, and of damp wood. Damp! In the most severe drought for twent-five years. The place was sinister, and not just because of what one human being was inflicting on another.

I came to Longbottom Lane and, looking across to the field on the other side, realized that the ground undulated there as well. In one of those hollows, only a few yards from the lane, the gunman had aimed at PC Ashmore but had missed him! At the edge of the wood, separated from the lane by the hedge, I sat on a log and waited while Mr Smith learned of new realities. I waited fifteen minutes. No sound reached me. Then I walked back.

Mr Smith was still locked to the tree. He was unconscious, head on chest, his face hidden from me. The handcuffs must have been tearing the flesh off his wrists. On the ground in front of him, close to his body, was a small grey mound which I at first assumed to be vomit. Then Jim, who had a fresh cigarette in his holder, suddenly swooped down, stirred the little mound with a short stick, extracted the glowing ember to light his cigarette. Then I understood why the ground at Mr Smith's knees was so churned up: evidence of further frantic attempts to back into the tree.

'You haven't — ' I said.

'Fried his sausage?' said Jim. 'No. He saw the point, as it were, long before that was necessary.' He laughed. 'What broke him up was the skilfully timed presentation of my warrant card. He was so relieved to discover we're all on the same side!' I stared at Jim. 'It seems that the current interest in the shooting incident is due to the fact they lost a very small quantity of arms in this area about two and a half years ago. An Armalite rifle was included.'

'Lost?' I said, managing the one word.

'Snatched, snitched or stolen. The timing of the event indicates the reason for Sir Gregory's resignation. The old fool committed the classic blunder for an administrator of getting himself directly involved in a field operation. As far as our Mr Smith is aware the cache of arms was being transported from

London to Portsmouth — for reasons for which I did not press him. It seems there was some kind of cock-up that prevented their team in Portsmouth taking delivery of the weapons on the date agreed. Somehow or other the big chief up at The Hall got himself involved; offered his place as hidaway *en route*. It was while the guns were at The Hall that they were stolen. Sir Gregory took the wise course of resigning before all the section heads could get together and persuade the PM to fire him. He had committed *the* crime in the Intelligence book by getting involved, never mind losing the guns.'

'But why the hell did he do it?'

'Dunno. Don't care really. Not interested in Intelligence history, are we? But guessing, I'd say he had a yen to get back in the field, prove something; show that the old dog still had teeth. He wouldn't be the first successful man to ruin himself for vanity.'

'Vanity?' I spoke as a child faced with a new word. But there was no time to speculate.

'I've radioed the van,' said Jim. 'You go back to the road and I'll clean up our friend here. Frimmer'll want the goods in decent condition.'

'Decent?' I said, sarcastically.

'Ah, fuck off!' said Jim, his manner ruffled for the first time. 'Don't make out I'm a monster. You wanted him to talk just as much as I did. *And* it serves him right. Keep your cards too close to your chest and you get your nipples twisted.' Mr Smith tried to raise his head, gave a sigh of pain. I left.

By the time I got back to the lane I was a bit more in control. Jim had read me correctly: my relief that *he* had done the persuading and not me. No adverse report by me! I already knew I was going to use the coward's way. It even had its own time-worn escape clause: acting on information received. No need to know how the information was obtained.

A small black Transit van edged its way along the lane, stopped ten yards from me. I did not know the driver but, to my astonishment, when he walked to the rear of the van and opened the doors,

Frimmer climbed out. I got the impression there was at least one other person with him in the back of the van. Frimmer strolled up to me, cigar clenched in his right fist.

'Afternoon, Bull.'

'Good afternoon, sir.'

'Thought I'd come myself just to say hello.'

Lying sod, I thought. Just trying to get his sticky fingers into the fieldwork. Vanity like Sir Gregory's. With a bit of luck the same outcome. Cut it out, Jack, or you're in trouble. 'Things may be moving,' I said.

'Tell me!'

So I told him, eagerly stealing the thunder from Jim Douglas. Somewhere behind me he was tidying up Mr Smith; perhaps, with a more subtle form of cruelty, implying to his victim that his troubles were not yet over.

'So,' said Frimmer. 'There may be some meat on the bone after all. What began as a propaganda exercise with the PM could *be* a murder case. Funny to think the local copper's notebook contained that vital bit of the jigsaw. Just think on that, Bull. If our Security colleagues had not been *so* security-minded Ashmore would've been directly involved and given them that idea. That's how narrow the margin by which SIU got into this.'

'But still no more than an idea about the dogs, sir,' I said.

'True enough, Bull. But DI Green will have told you I've designated this job a murder inquiry. We now have a link between Sir Gregory's death and the attempt on Ashmore that's a damned sight stronger than mere accident of geography. They are linked by that gun. That's not merely an idea, is it?'

'No, sir.'

'And I can tell the PM that not only did his Intelligence services carelessly allow themselves to be robbed of guns, but that one of the weapons was later used in an attempt to murder one of Her Majesty's police officers. Do us a power of good that will. Ah, here comes Douglas and friend.'

We watched the two men walk out of the wood and onto the lane. Mr Smith, hands now cuffed in front of his body, seemed dazed but unharmed. But as he walked to us the signs of his ordeal were more obvious. There was a clot of blood in his right nostril. The raw wound in his lip, where he had bitten it, was beginning to swell. The handcuffs appeared to be flecked with rust. And, although his clothing was decently arranged, the slash in the front of his trousers still gaped like a wound.

'You call this propaganda, sir? Hardly creditable for SIU is it?' I said.

'Don't worry your little head, Bull,' said Frimmer, sharply. 'By the time we've finished with him and are ready to hand him back he won't even remember this afternoon.' He turned his back on me, told Jim to put the victim in the van. As Mr Smith was led away he looked directly into my face. I feared that whatever awaited the poor devil back at SIU headquarters, he would *not* forget who had turned away from him in Swallows Wood. Frimmer turned to face me again.

'A word to the wise, Bull. When I put you on a case I get the feeling I'm unleashing rather than assigning you. It will make quite a change if you actually arrest someone this time. Your first jobs, counting the one in the States, only produced a lot of work for the coroner. Got me?'

'Yes, sir,' I said, stiffly. In the van a body fell heavily to the floor. At least two men laughed.

'I'll take DS Douglas up the road a bit and then drop him off. That way you and he won't be seen together.'

'Good,' I said, vehemently. But all Frimmer did was raise his eyebrows before turning away and walking to the rear of the van. The driver shut him in with Jim and Mr Smith and others, then walked to the cab. He opened the door, nodded at me as though to a stranger who had kindly given him directions for his journey. As the van drew away I started to walk in the opposite direction. The shorter route for me was through the wood and over the fields to Testem Magna, but I did not intend to walk again in Swallows Wood. Nor was it a fit place for a unicorn.

13

By the time I returned to the Wheatsheaf Mr Smith had been wiped out. His car had been driven away, and when I walked past the open doorway of his room I saw that his cases had gone and a chambermaid was stripping the bed. I went straight to my room, stripped naked, put on fresh clothes and then went for a long walk. When I returned I had a very deep hot bath.

Meeting Mrs Wentall in the bar at evening opening time I led the conversation to the fact Mr Smith's room was being cleaned.

'E's left, m'dear. Went off late this afternoon. He came in here about tea time, said he had to move on, collected his things, paid his bill.'

'*He* came in this afternoon?' I struggled to keep my voice even. While I had been tramping the countryside . . .

'Well — yes, sir. Anything wrong, sir?' I

133

was warned by the gleam in her eyes.

'No, not with me, Mrs Wentall. But at lunch time Mr Smith told me he felt unwell. I'm just a bit surprised by his leaving so soon.'

'Funny you should say that, sir. He didn't seem quite himself. His voice sounded funny — not that he said much. He was a quiet man anyway. Mr Wentall was only saying last night . . . '

I didn't listen any more. Knew how they'd done it. Taken a face moulding in the back of that van, coloured it up. Someone of similar build had worn it, come into the hotel, paid cash, cleared his things. No signatures required. And he hadn't talked much either. But there was one thing they couldn't wipe out.

I escaped Mrs Wentall, carried my beer toward the garden but via the front door. At the reception desk I picked up the register, checked for Mr Smith's name, address and signature. His entry should have been between Susie's and Jim's. No such entry, no blank space either: Jim's signature directly under Susie's. I lifted the book, held the page against the daylight from the glazed front door. No trace of anything rubbed out or lifted off the paper. I opened the pages wide and inspected the binding: no sign a page had been ripped out or a new one stitched in. I could feel the hair pricking on the back of my neck. I put the book down, turned it round so it faced away from me as I had found it. Once again I experienced the sensation of being held by an organization. I was relieved it was working with and not against me. And if Mr Smith, a senior field Intelligence agent is so easily 'eliminated' what chance has any opposition got? I picked up my beer, turned to the door. Susan Green was watching me through one of the small square windows. As I shook the spilled beer off my hand she opened the door and came in.

'Good evening, Dr Bull.' I nodded at her. As she stepped up to me she stared into my face. 'Trouble?'

'No,' I said. 'Everything according to plan. How about you?'

'I'll get a drink. Join you in the garden.'

Choosing a seat well out of sight of the

Testing Stone I gulped down some cold beer. Despite the shade thrown by the hotel buildings it was still very warm in the garden. The warmth now had a closeness, clamminess, reminding me of Swallows Wood.

'You first,' said Susie, sliding along the bench at the other side of the table.

'Science is marvellous, ain't it?' I said, raising my glass to her.

'The register? Oh, yes. Specially when it works *with* us.'

Yes, I thought, but there's still a place for old-fashioned torture.

'So what's your news, Jack?'

I told her the tale as if it had been told me by Jim Douglas who had long, long ago been told it by some mythical figure named Smith. Perhaps something in my manner warned her against enquiring after the health and welfare of Mr Smith. More likely, she simply didn't care. She had only two questions.

'How did Frimmer react to this breakthrough?'

'Like a greedy child that got its cake.'

'And do you agree, Jack, we tell PC

Ashmore about this?'

'Yes, I do. He's already compromised. No harm in telling this part of the story now he's guessed about the security angle. Besides, it's a sweetener. Let him feel he's joined the team. We may still need him.'

'Certainly we need him,' she said. 'He's agreed to be bait for a second time. No, save your questions. I'd rather deal with this new development when Jim's with us.'

'Jim?' I said, dismayed.

'He'll need briefing as well, won't he? What I'm arranging is that he and I come to your room this evening for a chat, and that I arrange to see Ashmore by himself somewhere else. That'll cut down our security problems a bit. Four's a crowd in this neck of the woods.' She put her empty glass down on the table.

'Another?' I said.

'Please. It's draught lager. When you come back I'll give you my impressions of your lady friend up at The Hall.'

In the bar Jim Douglas sat with his drink and read the evening paper. No grief pretending I did not know him.

'Jim's in the bar,' I said to Susie, putting our drinks on the table.

'Thought he was back. He'll have some things I ordered from Wilson and Stone. But that'll keep. You want to hear about Lady Fortis?'

I wasn't sure I was ready for that but I nodded, drank most of my beer.

'Well, she invited me to have afternoon tea with her.' I interrupted her to ask if Nicky was there. 'No sign. Saw James though; gorilla seems a fair description. I'd been in the study about an hour when he came shuffling up and made noises at me. I got the gist and followed him downstairs to the library. My dear, you should have seen: silver salvers, scones and cream, best silver teapot, and her ladyship presiding in a very expensive blood-red dress. Made this shirtwaister of mine look very ordinary. She was so friendly, so anxious to put me at ease, I went along with the charade. We talked about the weather, the house, the garden, how I enjoyed working for you. I began to wonder what she was up to. Then it clicked. She was desperate to spend time with someone nearer her own age, especially a woman. She's a few years older than me but at least I'm nearer her age than is her son. I think part of her trouble is being bored out of her mind living with a twenty year old motor biking kid. But when I led her onto the subject of Nicky she switched it round to talking about Sir Gregory; how good he'd been to the boy, how considerate, understanding etc. I might've swallowed her line except that when she poured me the second cup of tea she put a lot of it into the saucer. That elegant woman, handling a perfectly pouring teapot, couldn't hit the cup.

'So I kept things going, and what I picked up was some combination of anger and anxiety; not that I could work out where it all fits. Somewhere deep, very deep, she's angry with the boy, and it feels stronger than parental disapproval of a few wild parties and ripping up the countryside on a powerful bike.'

'Any grief?'

'Some, I think, but she's largely over

that. Something dismissive in the way she speaks of Sir Gregory. Even her praise of him felt — felt kind of second hand; praising him for how he accepted his stepson rather than for any specific virtues of his own. He is a kind of non-person in her memory; perhaps more than that — a non-person when alive. And when you think of who he was, what he achieved, the power he had, you realize what a powerful person *she* must be.'

'Capable of murder, Susie?'

'Most of us are. But, yes, no doubt about that. And she has that combination of great inner strength which is flawed by overstatement somewhere. You know the sort of thing I mean: the brilliantly successful businessman who's a miser; the saint who's unyielding to the point of cruelty.'

'What's the overstatement in her?'

'Something sexual.' We sat silent for a moment. 'You with me, Jack?'

'Yes. You're on target. It would also fit neatly with the theory that the local vet swapped the dogs because he was crazy about her. What promises, spoken or unspoken, had he picked up?'

'Right, Jack. Might also fit in another area as well: with Sir Gregory's apparent stupidity in getting involved in a field operation.'

'You don't go for vanity then?'

'On the contrary, Jack. How about the most powerful of all vanities: sexual vanity? At age 50 he married a widow age 32. Within three or four years he had to face the fact he couldn't cope with her demands. Maybe his sex drive was always low. After all, he could've married at 40, once he withdrew from field operations. His job did not preclude marriage. Anyhow, there he was, his self-confidence badly damaged by a woman whom I'm sure knows just how to twist the knife; his self-esteem also being trampled by watching his more youthful replacements in the field. Then, suddenly on his doorstep in an apparently harmless form, is a chance to pretend he's the one who's still in his mid-thirties; still a buck. He's hooked.'

'But Susie, all his years of experience — '

'Could be as nothing before the power of a woman!'

How could I argue with that, in the face of world history; in the face of Susie's beauty confronting me?

'Then he had the bad luck to have the guns stolen,' I said, trying to imagine how he must have felt when he discovered his loss.

'You think so? Don't we make our own luck, Jack?'

I didn't reply. I was trying to imagine the pressure on Sir Gregory; especially the scornful disparagement received from that powerful lady. But somehow something still didn't quite fit. I felt I was looking down on a jigsaw puzzle, the pieces all available but some not yet the right way up.

'And what was the anxiety you detected?' I asked.

'Maybe something about giving herself permission to spend time with me, with someone thought to be sane and of the world. Would I reassure her that she is sane as well or would I mirror some other view of her? Or maybe it's just something about her wild son.'

'Yeah. Odd contradiction there. The wild son needs all his gear on just to come down the drive and meet me.'

'Well, Jack, you ponder that one while I have my bath. I'll see you at dinner. Afterward, Jim and I will sneak into your room.'

I watched her walk away from me. My mind was partly occupied with jealousy that Jim would now be working more closely with her. But overriding those thoughts were my recollections of Isobel Fortis sitting beside me in that vulgar room, her dark head bowed over interlaced fingers. If good old solid, dependable, unexciting Sir Gregory was earth his woman was fire.

14

We met in my room as arranged. I was somewhat piqued by the proprietorial way Jim Douglas sat himself on my bed next to Susie. I stared out of the window at the Testing Stone. Above and beyond it the sky was clouding over for the first time since Susie and I had arrived two days ago. Only two days!

'Ready?' asked Susie. I sat down in the armchair facing her and Jim. 'You first,' she said to Jim.

'Here we are,' said Jim, pulling some photographs and folded typescript from his jacket pocket. 'Some further details of blameless pasts. Lady Fortis's first husband died of a heart attack. He had been in intensive care for three days before he died. There is no evidence whatsoever she hastened him on his way. Seems she played devoted wife perfectly. Stayed in a private room in the hospital, never got in the way of the nursing staff.

Genuinely grief-stricken when he died.'

'How about the son?' asked Susie.

'A non-runner also,' said Jim, slightly smug. 'He *is* her son, is legitimate, no criminal record, no record of mental illness. We knew most of this stuff before we got into the field but Frimmer is adamant that Mr Stone and staff get everything rechecked very thoroughly.

'As for the gorilla — '

'Had him included as well, did you?' I asked, staring at Susie.

'Everyone, Jack, everyone,' she said. 'Even Brad Ashmore, Mrs Ashmore, the Wentalls, the lady in the lodge house. You name 'em, Frimmer and Stone are checking or rechecking them.'

'As I was saying, my dears,' Jim was waspish. 'The gorilla, James Webb, also has nothing known but his background is a trifle seedy. Drifted from one job to another, became a bouncer at a London club, then a minder. It seems Nicky Fortis acquired him from the son of an Arab oil sheikh, when the son came down here to a party. Apparently, there was bother about how James Webb might fit in at Oxford when his young charge goes up later this year. Webb's been at The Hall since Easter.'

'So he never knew Sir Gregory,' I said.

'Right. He's also pretty thick and unlikely to be a useful conspirator in any plot. His main virtue, which a psychiatrist could explain, is total loyalty to his current paymaster.'

'Like us,' I said, maliciously. There was silence.

'Sod!' said Jim.

'So,' said Susie, rather loudly. 'How about our friendly vet, Barnard Hardwicke?'

'New photos,' said Jim, spreading them out on the floor. We leaned forward and looked at the new shots of that big, sad bloodhound of a man, his high domed balding head shining in the sunlight. 'Taken this morning,' said Jim in answer to my question. 'DCI Wilson sent Francis down with the photographic van and his newest camera. That one, for example, that head and shoulders, was taken at a range of three hundred yards.' We expressed ourselves impressed. I had a new vision of the countryside: every tree a policeman, every bush a camera, every stone a microphone.

'And his background?' asked Susie.

'Nothing really new turned up there. A blameless lad. Absolutely mother-ridden when young; encouraged to believe himself to be of a nervous disposition. Lived to that script even after Mummy died. But apparently showed some interest in women once the old bat was dead. Got himself registered with a reputable marriage bureau but nothing came of his various meetings. The rest of the stuff about him is in these notes Frimmer gave me, but there's nothing significant.'

'You've already said one of the things that matter,' I said. 'He sounds absolutely ripe for falling under the spell of a rich fascinating widow just a few years younger than himself.'

'That so,' said Jim, looking at Susie. Briefly, she told him of the ideas we'd been talking over before dinner. 'The theory is then,' said Jim, 'that Hardwicke, besotted by Lady Fortis, was persuaded to change the dogs on the fourth of January. That night they killed Sir

Gregory who was the only other person who could have identified the dogs. OK. So why didn't he?'

'Bitter cold, dark night, dogs made bad-tempered anyway by the cold — Dobermanns are short-coated — and he had no reason to suspect anything.' I shivered as I spoke. 'One Dobermann looks much like another and Hardwicke probably selected the substitutes with some care. Once Sir Gregory opened the gate of the kennel compound it was too late. Then Hardwicke himself set up the autopsy on those dogs. Ironic that PC Ashmore was partly responsible for that. As we know, the second vet called in had no reason to question the identity of the dogs lying on the slab. The final touch was burying them with their victim. Grave filled in — end of story. But some weeks later PC Ashmore quite unwittingly rattled Hardwicke. A few days afterward some panic-stricken character tried to shoot Ashmore as he cycled past Swallows Wood.'

'Almost likely — the way you tell it,' said Jim, grinning at me. 'Any other fairy story before I go to my bed?'

'Well, you know there's one about the erring Security chief put down by his own people,' I said.

'No hooks to hang that one on,' said Jim, breezily. 'Sir Gregory's resignation was all that his enemies required. Self-neutralization was quite enough to satisfy their blood lust. No doubt about it, the theory that looks promising is the domestic one; not that it's that sparkling an attraction.'

'But it's tenable, isn't it?' said Susie.

'As a theory,' said Jim. 'I guess Frimmer's done the right thing designating our operation a murder inquiry. But I also think he's right not to have told the PM he's done that. Less egg on his face if it gets nowhere. What's next?'

'It's already set up,' said Susie. 'While you two were bird-watching in Swallows Wood PC Ashmore put the frighteners on Hardwicke for the second time. He went to the kennels and asked some rather pointed questions about the amount of business Hardwicke was getting in the Dobermann market. He also let on that he was working on something of his own which he hadn't told anyone because it was not much more than a vague theory. Just to keep Hardwicke on his toes he let him know it was something to do with an event earlier this year.'

'Didn't know about this,' I said.

'Set it up with him yesterday when I got back from Salisbury and he returned from Acton Westhurst. No need for you two to know about it until now,' said Susie, firmly. 'But now you need to know the next bit as well. Our village bobby also confided in Hardwicke that tomorrow morning he'd be in Longbottom Lane beside Swallows Wood investigating a rumour about a man with a gun. He did not tell him that you two will be bodyguarding.'

'Thanks a lot,' said Jim.

'Brad Ashmore's not short of guts, is he?' I said.

'No,' she said. 'And it also seems appropriate he should have the chance to check out his own theory. There's another reason as well.' She paused. Jim and I looked at each other and then at her. 'He set something up last night,' she said in a neutral tone.

'What the hell does that mean?' asked Jim.

'After he met Jack and me at the Steelstones last evening and told us his idea about the dogs he then went on to The Hall.'

'Bloody hell,' I snarled. 'What's he up to?'

'He went up there and made sure he was seen by people arriving for the party. He told Nicky Fortis he was checking car numbers following reports of an accident. Our village bobby told me he did his best to make that sound unconvincing. He's determined to start a landslide somewhere.' Susie raised her right hand, checking my attempt to speak. 'No good any of us getting shirty, Jack. He's quite unrepentant. When he reported this to me earlier today he made it clear he intends to get very much involved in our inquiry. He's a very angry man. Waiting around for the last few weeks has really screwed him up. And who can blame him? So, setting him up tomorrow suits him, and helps us keep him close.'

'I just hope you're right about that — ma'am,' said Jim, standing up. 'I'm for a last drink and then bed. It begins to sound as if Jack and I will need our wits about us playing bodyguards to that lunatic. Anything else, ma'am?'

'Not now,' said Susie, also standing. 'Good night, gentlemen. See you at breakfast. I'll check the corridor's clear for you, Jim.'

When they had both gone I picked up the photographs and notes Jim had brought from DCI Wilson. I stared at the photographs of Barnard Hardwicke and he stared back at me. Poor little sod, I thought. More chewed up by women than dogs! I began to read through the notes. Halfway down the third page I stopped. Jim had said there was nothing significant. He could be wrong. Carrying the notes I walked out of the room, knocked on Susie's door.

'What the hell?' she said, letting me in.

'Lovely dressing-gown,' I said, ogling.

'Have you come in here to — '

'No,' I said, quickly. 'Not that I don't

want to. Work, I'm afraid.' We both grinned. I shut the door behind me.

'What is it then?' she said, sitting on the bed. I remained standing.

'You know Jim said there was nothing in these notes?'

'There is?'

'Could be a pointer, no more. Jim hasn't met Lady Fortis yet, has he?'

'No. Only seen the photos.'

'So maybe he didn't have the chance to make the connection I'm making.'

'Which is?' She was infected with my excitement.

'When Hardwicke signed with the marriage bureau he filled in a question-naire, and the photostat of it is in these notes. He had to specify the sort of woman he wanted to meet, and one of the questions asked for a physical description.'

'And?'

'He wrote: 'short, slim, dark with brown eyes. Age thirty-five to forty-five'.'

'Fits Isobel,' she said.

'Yes,' I said. 'No value as evidence but interesting tie-up. Adds spice for what we're setting up tomorrow.'

She gave me a strange look, hesitated before speaking. 'Take care with Hardwicke if he surfaces. He might be dangerous.'

'Yes, ma'am,' I said.

'Hear me!' she said, sharply. 'Just remember the risk he was prepared to take exchanging the dogs. We could be wrong to think it was simply part of the day's work to him. Maybe when he opened the cages he faced the same fate as Sir Gregory.'

'How so?'

'The dogs he meant to take away could have attacked him as ferociously as their replacements attacked Sir Gregory.'

'He could've tranquillized them first,' I said.

She stood up, stepped close to me. 'If that's the reality you want to believe, Jack,' she said. Then she kissed me on the mouth. 'I still say take care.'

Then, somehow or other, she bundled me out of her room and into the corridor. As she whispered good night I heard her slide the door catch into position.

15

Friday morning, lying behind the hedge in the young wheat in sunlight, I had *that* feeling: something wasn't going to work. I've learned the lesson every policeman has to learn: if an operation can be summarized in a few simple words then complications are guaranteed. And the words were simple.

'Between 10 a.m. and 12 noon, on Friday 8th May, PC Ashmore will patrol Longbottom Lane in the vicinity of Swallows Wood. During this time Detective Sergeants Douglas and Bull will keep watch from the west and east road junctions respectively. Both officers will be armed and carrying radios. Detective Inspector Green will be at The Hall on the pretext of continuing her research in Sir Gregory Fortis's study. She will also carry a radio and will inform DS Douglas and DS Bull if either Lady Fortis or Nicky Stapolous leave The Hall. DS

Douglas at the west end of Longbottom Lane, and in the position closest to Swallows Wood, will have use of his S.I.U. car. Whatever the outcome of the operation his first priority will be the safety of PC Ashmore. DI Green will have the Range Rover and will remain at The Hall unless an emergency arises. DS Bull will be on foot. PC Ashmore will have his bicycle. In the event of an incident occurring DS Douglas will drive toward Swallows Wood and block the road with his car. DS Bull will remain on station at the east end of Longbottom Lane to be joined by DI Green, who will drive down from The Hall as soon as she is informed by radio that an incident has occurred.'

These words, jotted down by Susie, had been read by Jim before breakfast, and by me at breakfast. Then the note had been sealed in an envelope and posted to SIU for the information of DCI Wilson and the self-protection of DI Green.

Maybe some quite different words had generated my uneasiness.

'I heard you shout in the night,' Susie

had said, putting mustard on a piece of sausage. I had explained about bad dreams, apologized for disturbing her. 'Comes of having our beds against the party wall,' she had said, a trace mischievously. Then she had asked about the dream.

So I had told her of the green snake which, when it coils itself round my chest, makes a sinister rasping noise with its scales as it twists and twines about me. Its intention is always the same: to crush the life from me. Until now I have thwarted it by waking in time.

'That's what this job does to you,' she had said.

'Makes me dream?'

'No, you fool. Crushes all the life, all humanity out of you.'

I had not replied. I knew she had guessed something of what had happened in Swallows Wood yesterday. Mr Smith would not have been so informative by choice. I also wondered if she knew the other and sexual interpretation of my dream.

Now, lying in the wheatfield behind the

hedge, I knew words were over. Some tragic and dreadful action was about to begin. Like an elderly tortoise I lifted my head above the green grain, looked once more toward the road junction that marked the east end of Longbottom Lane. The continuation of the lane led away on a curving route into undulating country to the south of me, toward Barnard Hardwicke's kennels and animal hospital. The road that came into the junction from the left was the route from Testem Magna and The Hall. That was the way Susie would come if we called her in. I had a very clear view of the T junction from my side of the hedge because I could see through the gap where the five-barred gate used to be. It had required all my strength to lift that gate off its hinges and lean it against the hedge at the lane side. If I needed to block off Longbottom Lane that gate would make a good barricade. I looked at my watch. 10.30. Another radio check.

Jim Douglas sounded half asleep but reported he could see PC Ashmore who was on foot and trundling his bicycle slowly along the lane past Swallows Wood and toward Jim's position. I switched off. Pointless to say how I felt about the whole business; tactless also with Susie listening in at The Hall. I put my radio down in the wheat, momentarily buried my face in my folded arms, felt the sun cuff the back of my neck, felt the parched ground burning beneath me. The breaking of meteorological records did not assuage my discomfort. That was when I first heard the motor bike.

It was so far away I nearly disbelieved. Then I knew it was being driven toward me; the engine note regular but the volume rising as the bike approached from the south. South! Barnard Hardwicke?

I grabbed my radio, called Jim. He said he could hear it as well but it was still far away. No reply from Susie. The light on her radio must have come on but someone must have been nearby to prevent her switching on sound and acknowledging.

'Getting nearer,' I said to Jim. 'Can't wait on DI Green. Out!' I pushed myself tight into the hedge, watched the road from the south. I wondered if Nicky Stapolous was on the prowl, had slipped away from The Hall without Susie knowing. No time to check. The volume was swelling ominously as the bike approached me. I do not know why I drew my pistol at that moment. For all I knew some little old lady was approaching in a souped-up invalid chair. Not true. I knew the sound was wrong for that.

Then the sound was wrong for everything. The volume was constant. And I was back in the Range Rover with Susie on Tuesday afternoon and the sky was falling on my head. Constant volume: constant distance. Just like Tuesday and the bastard was riding *round* me. I snatched at the radio.

'Look out, Jim! He's not on the road but riding round me. He's coming cross-country. Close in on Ashmore!' As I spoke I was turning away from the lane and facing into the wheatfield. About four hundred yards away from me, beyond the rise in the ground, dust was rising.

Then he was in view on the rise, black

against the bright southern sky. He was not driving toward me but was going to pass me at a distance of about one hundred and fifty yards and travelling obliquely away from me. Helmeted, visored, alien. It was only the rifle strapped across his back that told me he was of this earth. And Bradford Ashmore — plodding beside his new bike, his symbol of earthly survival — had no time left.

I sprang to my feet, began to run along the edge of the field parallel to the hedge and to Longbottom Lane behind it; the lane on which Brad was pacing his last strides. As I began to run the motorcyclist switched off his engine. He intended to roll silently down the field and onto the lane. I ran faster, heard myself cursing, pleading with the motorcyclist to see me in time, to turn away. Part of my mind knew that my radio was on and that my colleagues could hear me cursing as I ran. Then I realized the gap between myself and the motor-cyclist was increasing. Without thought or hesitation I fired three shots into the air.

Rolling with engine off, the rider heard

my shots, looked back over his shoulder. Then he was revving the engine, slamming in the gears, turning away and accelerating fiercely, rear wheel ripping out the young wheat.

'Get him, Jim,' I gasped and fell into the hedge. Out of my radio came Jim's curses as he ran back to the car. Beneath his voice was Susie's anxious query about the shots. Then, a moment filled only by the revving of the motor bike and its harsh rasping progress over the wheat.

Jim did his best but by the time his red car burst spectacularly into the field the motor-cyclist was half a mile ahead and racing toward some distant gateway. Once on the road there would not be even a tyre track to follow. Jim would not overhaul him and Susie would not get down from The Hall in time to join the chase. As Jim gave up, turned the car back toward Longbottom Lane, I began to walk along the edge of the field toward a point opposite Swallows Wood. I was halfway there when the Range Rover slewed to a halt on the far side of the hedge.

'Get in!' Susie ordered, hard-faced.

'For Christ's sake!' said Jim, as we drew up next to his dust-caked car. He was standing in the road leaning against the open door.

'Don't bother!' said Susie to him, as she and I stepped down onto the road. 'Jack knows what he's done.'

They both stared at me. We stood between the cars each daring the other to speak. Then the silence was broken by the ringing of a bicycle bell. We watched PC Ashmore slowly ride past. He nodded gravely in our direction. The expression on his face was enough. The smart-arses from the big city had blown it.

'Didn't you see or hear Nicky Stapolous set out?' I said to Susie, partly to defend myself against the silence.

'When I got into the Range Rover Nicky Stapolous was sitting in the backyard with pieces of motor bike all round him.' I could feel my jaw dropping. 'You fool, it wasn't Nicky Stapolous. He's not the only motor-cyclist around here. And you — ' she jabbed a finger at Jim — 'get your car rolling, collect that cocky copper off his bike and go down to Hardwicke's place. Move it! Forget about your cover. Too late for that!'

Jim dived into the car, reversed it fiercely back into the hedge, swung clear of our car and raced after PC Ashmore. As Susie and I coughed in the dust and fumes she signalled me to get into the Range Rover.

'About all you and I can do is protect our own cover. I can tell them at The Hall I rushed out because I'd overlooked an appointment with you for 10.30 at the Steelstones. As I drive us up there you can explain exactly what you thought you were doing.'

So while she drove I told her what I had thought I was doing and she didn't hear me.

'But we *wanted* him to attack PC Ashmore,' she said, exasperated.

'Attempt,' I said. 'Attempt. The way he was coming in over the field made me think he might succeed.'

'So?' she said, harshly. 'Ashmore was prepared to take that risk. It wasn't even an issue for *you*. But you decided to take

164

it upon yourself and bugger up the whole thing.'

'I wasn't going to stand by — '

'That is exactly what you were required to do and you hadn't the guts to carry it through. All right, Sergeant! It was on for either you or Douglas to intervene at the very last moment to save a life, but our suspect never even got within sight of his target. If you can't get to grips with your anxiety state you're out of SIU. Thanks to you we're left with a trespassing motor-cyclist, carrying a fishing rod that looks like a gun, who halfway across a short cut remembered he'd left the kettle on the stove. Not quite the outcome we were seeking.' There was a long silence.

'But we know it wasn't Nicky Stapolous,' I said, trying to salvage something

'Thanks to me,' she said, tartly, swinging the car into the Steelstones car park. 'Now we spend the next couple of hours up here making sure our cover holds. Meanwhile, Jim Douglas has lost his. He now has to be CID assigned to PC Ashmore in further investigation of that original shooting. That'll make it that much more difficult for us to work with him. Before we get out of the car, check your gun and radio.'

'Fired three,' I said.

'You'll have to collect some from me this lunchtime. And the radio?'

'OK. Do I call Jim?'

'You've stirred up quite enough this morning. Wait until he calls us.'

Half an hour later, while holding up a ranging rod for Susie to focus on, I heard the muffled note of the radio bleeper in my pocket. I walked across to one of the largest stones so I was shielded from a group of hikers walking past. I took out the radio. Susie, guessing what had happened, left the theodolite and came and stood beside me.

'A blank,' said Jim. 'Hardwicke's out on his rounds in his car according to his staff. No sign of bike or gun. I've got the feeling a search warrant would be wasted. If the rider was Hardwicke he must've kept bike and gun somewhere else. Now we're just cruising the lanes.'

'Right,' said Susie. 'You've met his staff, probably driven past some locals as well. You're blown. Keep away from us. Stay in the open with PC Ashmore. You're CID down here on some official pretext. Got that? Don't contact us again unless absolutely vital. Radio preferred.'

'And?' said Jim.

'Put yourself in the gunman's place. What would you do after only just avoiding a trap — and someone fired shots as well?'

'OK, ma'am. But what about Bull's cover?'

'I doubt if the rider had long enough at that distance to recognize him.'

'Is he there?'

'Yes, Jim,' I said.

'Thank you so bloody much, Jack! Out!'

16

'Disgraceful I call it,' said Mrs Wentall, hauling in her bust on folded arms.

'Now my love,' said Mr Wentall, suspiciously soft as he handed me my drinks. 'No cause to bother Dr Bull.'

'Mebbe not,' she said, glowering.

'What's happened, Mrs Wentall?' I asked, desiring belief in my innocence. Mrs Wentall sighed heavily.

'That Mr Douglas who was here — the double glazing man on holiday — '

'Yes?'

'He's packed and left — just like that. Told Mr Wentall he's a policeman and that 'e's moving in with our PC Ashmore and his wife. Damned cheek!'

'Now, now,' said Mr Wentall, in his soothing-a-drunk voice. 'I know 'e's the second guest we've seen go off sharpish this week and that's upsettin'. But *that* isn't our business, my dear, not police business.'

'Not so sure about that. Him staying in our hotel pretending what 'e wasn't. What's it say about us, that's what I'd like to know?' She was beginning to strangle herself with her bust.

'He didn't look like a policeman,' I said, unwisely.

'Well 'oo does, these days?' she said, ferociously.

'I must take these drinks out to my assistant,' I said, backing away.

In the garden was Susie, thirsty but unsympathetic.

'New experience for you?' she asked, acidly, as I reported Mrs Wentall's anger.

'What is?'

'Taking an action absolutely no one at all is pleased about?'

I stuck my head over my tankard. No point at all in suggesting PC Ashmore might be 'pleased' with me. Alive he was but the expression on his face as he had ridden past us in Longbottom Lane had been neither congratulatory nor grateful.

'After lunch,' she said, 'you and I return to the Steelstones. Show ourselves in familiar activity in the same place, confirming identity. We need a damn' sight more to go on before we break *our* cover.'

'I hear a motor bike,' I said. 'Perhaps we have no cover left.' We waited. Sound grew hideous.

The motor-cyclist parked his machine on the other side of the hedge. He took off his helmet: Nicky Stapolous. Scowling, looking neither left nor right, he marched into the Wheatsheaf by the front entrance. We sipped our drinks. Waited.

A few minutes later he reappeared, looked over the hedge into the garden, acknowledged no one. He replaced his helmet, flicked at his leathers with his gloves, put his gloves on. Then he kicked the machine into life, roared off, leaving us and half a dozen locals, shaking our heads against the noise. I imagined that, out of sight round the corner, the Testing Stone must be rocking.

'Bloody yob!' someone said.

'Hush it!' said someone else. Six pairs of eyes flickered over us, dismissed us.

'A telephone report wasn't enough for him this time,' said Susie.

'You think the Wentalls've been on the phone again?'

'Seems likely. They were certainly best placed to describe your appearance when you went up to The Hall on Wednesday afternoon. Now they've had to tell him they've had a policeman under their roof, and that he's still lurking in the village.'

'Maybe the news'll encourage Nicky or someone to do something hasty.'

'I'd be happier to accept that remark as prophecy if I could be sure you weren't talking about yourself.'

'Susie!'

'OK, Jack. Truce declared. Let's eat.'

We ate and didn't talk: part sulking, part preoccupation. My preoccupation was with suspicion that the village and The Hall were linked in some kind of conspiracy, and that the pub was an information centre. But that was the pattern in many English villages; a network of gossip, subservience and time-serving that had nothing criminal in it. The Wentalls probably kept the Fortis family, and other wealthy families, up to date with village news as a kind of *quid*

171

pro quo for their custom. But was it coincidence the telephone line to The Hall was the one that was busy?

By 2.30 p.m. Susie and I were back at work as archaeologists at the Steelstones. In almost a dreamlike state we continued the exercise of surveying the circle. God knows what a real surveyor would have made of our efforts but we plodded on under the uncritical eyes of a handful of tourists. The warmth of the afternoon settled upon us; full stomachs making us even dreamier, even slower.

Occasionally, fair weather cumulus separated us from the sun but these temporary respites changed the light without lowering the temperature. Squinting through the theodolite at Susie I felt my eyelids hanging like heavy curtaining before a stage. A cloud crossed the sun and my eyes refused to adjust. Susie blurred; I yawned. As the sky grew darker, as cloud thickened, I struggled to stay awake. Susie, who was dressed in white T shirt and white jeans, was bright as a sword against the sky. I blinked, adjusted the theodolite away from her face and onto the rod she was holding vertically in front of the largest stone in the circle. The orange-brown of the stone, the soft greys of the lichens on its shady side, were too light against the sky. Something wrong. I blinked, shook my head, realized I had displaced the theodolite. I was again looking into Susie's lovely face framed by the blonde wig: gold halo separating her face from the dark cloud. Not cloud!

'Susie,' I hissed, raising my head. 'Look behind you!'

As she turned, I began to walk toward her. Behind her that dark cloud was rising higher. Less than two miles away in the lowland a fire was raging. I stood next to her.

'Binoculars in the car,' she said.

Obediently, I trotted down the slope toward the car park, but we already knew where the fire was. By the time I returned with the binoculars Susie had checked by radio that Jim Douglas and Brad Ashmore were on their way.

'They set out as soon as someone reported the fire,' she said, focusing the

glasses on the blaze. 'Here — you look.'
As she spoke the mournful sound of
fire-engines drifted up the hillside.

I focused. Barnard Hardwicke's house
and kennels sprang up like a toy village.
The flames were clearly visible at the base
of the oily black cloud.

'Looks like the fire's near the animal
crematorium,' I said, handing back the
glasses. 'Appropriate.'

'Yes,' she said. 'I can pick out the house
clearly enough as being this side of the
fire. Seems not to be involved at all.'

'Do we go?' She gave me a look. 'No, I
mean as sightseers.'

'Archaeologists don't do that,' she said.
'Back to work.' Twenty minutes later
patience was rewarded. Jim Douglas
called up on the radio, suggested that if
we would like a cup of tea with Mrs
Ashmore we could approach the cottage
on foot and unseen through the copse at
the rear.

'Serious enough to risk it?' asked Susie.

'Deadly,' said Jim.

'OK. Out,' said Susie to Jim. All three
of us switched off. 'Pack up,' said Susie to

me. 'Then get the very large-scale map of the village from the car.'

Debbie Ashmore, a dark-haired, rounded, smooth-skinned apple of a country-woman, opened her kitchen door to us as we walked quickly down the back garden path of her isolated cottage. She was not pleased to see us, made no response to our good afternoons. Her lower lip sank into a disfiguring pout. I saw her as she will be in forty years; that smooth skin raddled down to the texture of used tissue paper; cheeks falling into dewlaps. Resentfully, she showed us into the rear dining room, overlooked only by her garden and the trees beyond. Jim Douglas was sitting on an upright chair drinking tea.

'Thank you, Mrs Ashmore,' he said, firmly. Crossly, she shut the door. 'Brad's still at the fire,' said Jim, to us. 'Some tea?'

'Is she . . . ?' asked Susie, gesturing at the door.

'Have to assume she's discreet, don't we?' said Jim, shrugging. 'Not many places you and I can meet now, is there?' He favoured me with a cold look. 'No, I guess she's all right. She knows about the shooting business with her old man. So I laid it on a bit thick: she has his life in her hands — or mouth as it were. Took the point.'

'The fire?' asked Susie, accepting her cup of tea.

'The suicide,' said Jim, quietly. He allowed himself a moment to enjoy the expressions on our faces. Something in Susie's expression warned him about delaying too long.

'Yes,' said Jim, 'Barnard Hardwicke has hanged himself from the first floor landing banister rail in his home. His feet are twelve inches clear of the downstairs hall floor. Nearby, lying on its side, is the chair he kicked away.'

'Genuine?' I asked, wrestling with something like disappointment. Barnard Hardwicke was a key figure in this case and now I would never meet him. (But I hadn't met Sir Gregory Fortis either.) Somehow the case felt eerie, as if I didn't belong in it, didn't fit. It was a shadow play and I had no shadow. *That* was something like the feeling I had had when

I first met Lady Fortis.

'Looks genuine,' said Jim, hesitantly. 'No marks inconsistent with suicide as far as I could tell from the brief inspection I was allowed.'

'Allowed?' Susie's voice rose.

'Our PC Ashmore is playing this absolutely straight. Best thing he can do, ain't it?' We both nodded. 'He's keeping everyone at arm's length and has sent for further assistance. He hopes to join us here soon. There's a suicide note by the way.'

'Tell us,' ordered Susie.

Jim Douglas produced a crumpled piece of paper from his pocket. 'Ashmore wouldn't let me touch it but I was able to make this shorthand copy. Here goes.'

I have decided to end it all. I got in too deep. This morning I realised I could never get free. I confess that I caused the death of Sir Gregory Fortis by substituting three other Dobermanns in place of his own guard dogs. His dogs I put down and then disposed of in the crematorium. It was entirely my idea, my plan. Being a vet and also a breeder of Dobermanns I needed no help. No one else was involved in any way. Do not try to blame them. I am very sorry. There is no other way left now.

Barnard Hardwicke.

We sat and thought about the note for some time. Eventually, Jim spoke again.

'He sent all the staff home at lunchtime. Apparently, that was unusual. He must've done it then.'

''*This* morning I realised . . .'' quoted Susie.

'So perhaps he was the motor-cyclist,' I said, glumly.

'And the fire?' asked Susie.

'In the animal crematorium,' said Jim. 'It seems as if he was trying to destroy something and the fire got out of hand. In fact, the little chimney fell down while the brigade was putting out the flames.'

'Any idea?' I asked.

'Only guessing,' said Jim. 'But the fire chief says it looks as though some kind of explosion caused the fire to spread and get out of control.'

'Ammunition?' I asked.

'Possible,' said Jim. 'But we'll have to wait for all that.'

Then we heard voices in the hall.

'Maybe not much longer,' I said.

17

Sweating and triumphant, PC Brad Ashmore came into the room. Trying not to smile he towered over us all. His resentments of us, our power, our invasion of his home, were all brushed aside by the stench of success. I suspected we all felt sorry for him at that moment.

'Sit down in your own home, Brad,' said Susie.

'Thank you, ma'am.' He stripped off his uniform jacket, wiped a handkerchief over his face smudging smuts into his damp skin.

'Tea's still hot,' I said.

'Good,' said Brad, sitting down, seizing the teapot. 'Not only the fire was hot. Weather's turning muggy. Could be a storm at last. Please our farmers.'

'So what else is new?' asked Jim Douglas.

'It's likely we've cracked it — or rather you have,' said honest Brad. His world, unlike ours, was still framed within a simplicity I did not want to damage. I hoped he would never consider applying to join SIU.

'Start with the fire,' said Susie.

'Very fierce,' exclaimed Brad, spooning sugar into his tea. 'Possibly, petrol was used, maybe also pieces of rubber — a spare motor bike tyre perhaps.' He enjoyed our surprise while he gulped tea. 'It does appear he tried to burn, or at least remove evidence from, a gun. He must've known the metal parts would survive, of course. It is probable he hadn't realized, or just didn't care about, how much damage the ammunition might do. The side of the crematorium chamber was blown out and the fire spread to the whole building. He may have burned other things as well — documents perhaps. But we have to wait for Forensic to report.'

I had a picture then of poor demented Barnard Hardwicke pushing a rifle into the crematorium chamber knowing it would not be consumed but hoping to burn off evidence of ownership that might link it with his cold, unknowing lady. No, I thought, not unknowing. His unspoken love must have shone like a beacon in darkness. It would not be difficult to hate her.

'You reckon this closes the case?' asked Jim, maliciously. I wanted to help Brad but Susie got there first.

'What do you make of the note?' she asked. Perhaps she was offering Brad a second chance to avoid a mistake. I doubted if that possibility even flickered through his mind. He was focused on his biggest case being concluded.

'It confirms my theory about changing the dogs,' he said, eagerly. (Not only had his visitors got things wrong this morning, he was now able to claim getting them right two days ago.)

'Yes it may,' said Susie, quietly. She looked thoughtfully at Jim, then at me. He and I had every intention of sheltering behind her rank. 'What was the point of Hardwicke's reference to 'this morning'?'

'Well, ma'am, either he means that it was this morning he came to accept the full import of what he had done or he was the man on the motor bike.' His triumph was now so brightly shining we all guessed what he was holding back from us. 'I found a partly dismantled motor bike in his barn. No plates. It looks like he started on the plan of destroying it and then just lost heart. He must've either just bought it or stole it. I would not have overlooked his ownership of a bike. I miss very little on my patch.'

'Could he have been our mystery motor-cyclist on the day we arrived?' I asked.

'That is indeed possible, Sergeant. It seems of little significance now.' PC Bradford Ashmore was getting just a little above himself. I could share in Jim's desire to cut him down.

'Anything else?' asked Susie, hastily.

'Don't think so, ma'am. Of course, none of this is yet confirmed, not even that the note's in his handwriting. But it all fits, doesn't it?'

'Let's hope Forensic can prove he wrote that note,' I said, acidly. Then as Brad's face began to pucker with questions, I added: 'Otherwise your theory about changing the dogs will stay theory. The only two people who might prove it for you are now both dead as are *both* sets of dogs.'

There was a silence. A slight crease appeared on his forehead just above the bridge of his nose. For the first time his exhilaration did not deafen him to what it was we had said and not said.

'We're not missing anything, are we?' he asked, slightly truculent.

'*We're* not,' said Jim, spitefully.

'About the note,' said Susie, quickly. 'What do you think he meant about not blaming anyone else?'

'We — ell,' said Brad, suddenly uncertain. 'That no one else was involved. Perhaps — perhaps he means it was unrequited love or something; that Lady Fortis had no idea what he was up to?'

'But the note doesn't say 'she', it says: 'Do not try to blame *them*.' That right, Sergeant?' asked Susie looking at Jim.

'Yes, ma'am,' said Jim, curtly. Use of his rank had warned him off the clever stuff.

'But that could mean anything, ma'am,' said Brad. 'Could mean don't blame his kennel staff for leaving him alone when he sent them all away for lunch at the same time today, instead of the usual staggered arrangement.'

'Or maybe the 'them' is the 'they' *you* talked about up at the Steelstones the other evening,' I offered. 'When you said '*they* changed the dogs'.'

'Is it?' said Brad, now feeling confused.

'If it isn't, then we are saying that Barnard Hardwicke committed the murder, attempted to murder you, set out for a second attempt on you this morning, and did all that by himself.' Brutally, Susie put this summary to him, softening it only by the use of 'we' instead of 'you'.

'But surely that's possible, ma'am?' asked Brad. He pushed his teacup to one side as if clearing away confusion. Then he rested his elbows on the table, his chin in his cupped hands. 'It is possible,' he said, slightly more firmly. The frown was deeper, angrier. At exactly the moment of the case triumphantly closing his visitors were trying to force it open again.

'Yes,' I said. 'It is possible. But where did he get the gun?'

'Dunno,' said Brad, sullenly. 'Stole it?'

'Maybe,' I said. 'We believe it was stolen from the boot of Sir Gregory Fortis's car over two years ago.'

'Is that so?' Brad spoke very slowly, spacing the words with his anger at yet another piece of information previously withheld.

'Not sure,' I said. 'But if true how could he possibly have known it was in the car on that one particular day or night — unless *they* told him, or perhaps even stole it themselves.'

'So who are they?' said Brad, slapping his hands flat on his own table.

'Who's left alive?' asked Jim, grinning at him. 'Think about it, Brad.'

While he thought and I sat silent in the armchair, Susie sent Jim out of the house to check that the way was clear for her and me to slip away into the copse at the end of the back garden. She also wanted Jim out of Brad's hair. Rather plaintively, Brad asked her what he should do next. He seemed further disconcerted by her answer that he must concentrate on the Hardwicke suicide.

'No need to contact DS Bull and me unless there's a strong indication it wasn't suicide. We'll stay under cover for just a little longer; there may be some advantage left in that.'

When Jim returned Brad escorted Susie and me from his house and along the back garden path. No sign of his wife but I suspected she watched us from an upstairs window. I walked at the rear, unaware of any farewells that were spoken. Barnard Hardwicke's action had not only removed him from the scene, it had also transferred to others the focus of my attention. The need for speed, for a quick riposte after his death, had put me in a state not of anxiety but of disassociation. As Susie and I walked the pleasant woodland path to where we had tucked the car away in a field, I felt I floated slightly ahead of us, consciousness in the heavy clouds gathering above the downs. It was possible we now had two links: dogs and gun. Yet somehow the dogs remained the *crucial* link. They connected Sir Gregory with Barnard Hardwicke and with the man who had destroyed them: Nicky Stapolous. The ambiguity of that last sentence hit me.

I stopped walking. Susie also stopped, looked back at me over her shoulder, turned. 'Jack?' she said, very softly, correctly reading the dreamy expression which she later told me distorted my face like a gargoyle.

'Yes,' I said. 'Exhumation of the dogs.'

'But we've already — '

'No,' I said. 'Don't dismiss. Stay with it. What would we gain by doing that now?'

'Even less than before,' she said, still speaking softly, trying to edge into my mind.

'But what did we hope for *then*? I know it seems silly but what was the hope *about* — never mind its feebleness?'

'Someone would recognize the dogs as not being Sir Gregory's?'

'Right, Susie. But little chance of that; little chance of rattling Hardwicke on that, was there? None at all now. So what the hell am I after?' I started walking again, hardly aware I had put my arm round her waist and that she had not rebuffed me. That was a measure of how far gone I was! 'It *is* those damned dogs! Something about them. Let me stay with that.'

We walked on in silence. My absorption partly (partly) explained how I stayed with the embrace. Later, I wondered why she had made no attempt to release herself. I would like to think it was a reflection of our deep feelings for each other. I'd even settle for embrace as expression of forgiveness for the morning cock-up. Ha! But I stayed with the dogs all the way to the car, all the way to the Wheatsheaf and up the stairs to my room. I stared out at the Testing Stone and it stared back at me, its surface rippling alive under cloud shadows.

'Susie' I said. She was leaning against the doorframe watching me. 'I think it's going to rain at last. And I've got it! That is it! God almighty, how obvious a thing is when you see it. About the dogs. Obvious now. It's the bullets, Susie!' She hastily shut the door as my voice began to rise. 'Sorry,' I said. 'Somewhere I've read or heard that the dogs were not much cut up by the shooting. At almost point-blank range? So what gun did Nicky Stapolous use?'

'No need to shout,' she said. 'But go on.' She came and stood next to me on my left.

'He shot those dogs with a high-powered rifle: the Armalite. A shotgun at close quarters would've ripped them to pieces. Imagine buckshot hitting dogs at distances between two and twenty yards!'

'The reference you want is in one of those reports we read in the bunker,' said Susie. 'I remember it.'

'Me too — now. Susie, I've got it. The exhumation we need is not of the dogs but of the *bullets*. But at the range the dogs were killed those bullets passed straight through and into the ground of the dog compound. No wonder they were keen on grassing everything over.

'Now I understand something else as well. It wasn't only fastidiousness that made Nicky drag the dogs away from his stepfather's body. He also covered them up. Why? Then he locked 'em up. Why? Because he must've realized too late their corpses didn't 'look right'. A knowledgeable copper or ambulance man would've seen at once they'd not been hit with pellets. No wonder they were buried under Sir Gregory. Oh, bright lad, Nicky! But I think I've got you now!'

'But if Nicky had the gun he was the one who took the shot at PC Ashmore.'

'Yes, my lovely, gorgeous, senior colleague. Maybe *he* did. And poor old Hardwicke never got involved in any of that part of it until pushed into it now — this week, presumably by Nicky Stapolous. The young sod might even have hoped for the suicide as well.'

'Or helped?'

'Not directly.' I sat on the bed, took a deep breath. 'This clears up a coupla things I've been stuck with. That question I asked Frimmer at the briefing, and the thing I got about exhumation. Great!'

'That old black magic . . . ' she said, grinning.

'However much I trust my intuition, it's always a relief to find it confirmed.'

'Don't be too quick, Jack,' she said. 'It's not confirmed yet.'

'It will be once we get a metal-detector on that new grassland round The Hall. Tell you the other idea I'm enjoying: you and I can't do that if we mean to keep our cover. We stick the job on Jim Douglas, and while he's working away at it we sit in The Hall with Isobel and drink tea.'

'Something more important in The Hall than tea,' said Susie.

'Spoil-sport,' I said.

'Motive,' she said.

'Madam, I cannot accomplish everything at once. For me to try and intuit motive will require more time, patience and a very good wine at dinner.'

'My guest,' she said.

A vivid flash of lightning illuminated the room. For a moment she held my hand as the first great roll of thunder came out of the hills and down onto Testem Magna.

18

The violent overnight rain had subsided to a miserable drizzle that puckered itself on the window panes, distorting the view. Susie and I sat in Sir Gregory's study on the pretext of working. We were waiting for our colleagues to arrive with their metal-detectors.

'Will they work in the rain?' asked Susie, standing at the window, squinting out across the stable yard and grounds, across the belt of new grassland where the kennels had stood.

'Local police or metal-detectors?' She scowled at me. 'Suppose so,' I said, hastily. 'They use 'em on beaches, other damp places. We'll find out soon enough. It's 10.30.'

'Prop the door open,' she said.

I walked across the room, quietly opened the door. James Webb was standing on the landing looking down the stairs. He turned to face me.

'It's very warm in here,' I said. He glared at me. 'Yes,' I said, more firmly than I felt. We stared at each other. Then he dropped into a crouch and ambled toward the stairs. Seven steps down he looked back at me over his shoulder. 'See you later,' I said, cheerfully, and backed into the room. 'James,' I said to Susie.

'On guard?'

'Perhaps. Could raise a question. But maybe it's just that he's seen too many thirties films about family retainers.'

'He thinks we'll steal the family silver?' said Susie, smiling.

'Nah,' I said, rather loudly. Then I stopped and wondered why I was so sure. James on guard meant one of two things: mistrust of us or Fortis guilt. And I was dismissing mistrust without taking time to think about it. Maybe our cover had not held. Or if Lady Fortis had developed her intuition as much as I had my own, what did she intuit about me? Thoughts were interrupted.

The tinny notes of the vulgar door chimes echoed in the great entrance hall. We both trotted to the study door, stood back out of sight of the hall below. A housemaid answered the door, was brushed aside by James. An argument developed between him and the callers. We recognized Brad Ashmore's voice. Brad uttered a statement. James blocked it with a grunt. Brad tried again. Blocked. There was mention of a warrant. Warrant was produced. It sounded as if James had eaten it. Then Jim Douglas spoke for the first time. 'I think we must see Lady Fortis.'

James strung several grunts together, stamped across the hall. Susie and I leaned against each other, shaking with laughter.

'What the fuck is this about?' Nicky's voice came blasting up out of the hall, echoing and slapping its way up the marble staircase. Susie and I stepped apart. Brad began to explain but Nicky cut him short as soon as the warrant was mentioned. His voice became shriller. Every attempt Brad made to speak was shouted down.

For Susie and me the experience of eavesdropping was illuminating, if that doesn't sound double Dutch. Because we could not see the speakers we had to work only with aural signals. I realized I could hear the feelings behind the words in a quite different way, almost as if the people were subtly different as well. Not seeing the persona one began to hear the voice of the shadow: Brad apprehensive, Nicky angry.

Nicky's anger was underlain by the shrieking sounds of fear. No, more than fear. Fear in Nicky was a mutter; it is panic that shrieked with him. He was edging into panic. If he was pushed a bit harder he might respond in a way that made all subsequent investigation merely corroboration. But I suppose Brad and Jim couldn't 'hear' that as clearly as I did perched on the landing. They were trying to cope with all the visual signals as well. Stolidly, Brad ploughed into the script he had acquired for dealing with irate gentry. Susie and I looked at each other as the volume of sound increased. Blows were imminent. Jim must have picked up a slightly different signal.

'Shut up — sir!' he roared. The domed roof resonated the sound away. There was a moment of silence. 'Quite simple, sir,' added Jim, more quietly. 'We have a warrant, and there's only one alternative to that.'

'And that is?' asked Nicky, suddenly ice to Jim's fire.

'Your arrest, sir.' Whatever the young master might have said to that was never uttered. Another voice, colder than anything previously heard in that marbled hall, cut into the argument.

'Arrest? What are you talking about?' Lady Fortis had at last emerged from the library. Good timing. While we had been waiting for her son to spill something she must have been waiting for PC Ashmore to do so. Deadlock required her intervention.

'Good-morning, madam,' said Brad, calmly. 'We have a search warrant and your son is being obstructive.' There was another silence. Then Lady Fortis recovered sufficiently to speak, but her voice was suddenly unsteady.

'What is wrong?' She sounded breathless. 'What is wrong in my home?'

'Not the house, madam,' said Brad. (I

could've strangled the unimaginative sod!) 'We wish to search the grounds.' Another silence. Perhaps that was the moment in which her darkest, most dread suspicion was confirmed.

'In the vicinity of where your husband died.' Jim's voice slapped viciously against the walls, across her face.

'But — ' she said.

'What are you looking for?' asked Nicky, voice soaring in panic.

'Cause of death,' said Jim, brutally.

'But my husband — ' began Lady Fortis.

'Not your husband, madam,' said Jim, softly, 'his dogs.'

'But you *know* I shot the dogs,' cried Nicky.

'We know that, sir,' said Brad, in his role of quiet man. 'What we are not sure of is which gun you used.'

'Constable, I just grabbed a gun from the rack, for Christ's sake! I don't even have a very clear recollection of putting it back!'

'Really, sir?' said Brad. 'Well our problem is that we have instructions to search for a gun stolen a long time ago in this district. As a result we require to inspect that area where you shot the dogs. We need to find any expended ammunition or cartridge cases.'

'This is crazy,' said Nicky, his voice shaking.

'There is an alternative if you prefer it, sir,' said Jim. 'We can seek an exhumation order on the dogs.'

Lady Fortis made a gasping sound. It was Nicky who spoke, the words dragged out of him.

'But they're buried with, underneath — '

'We know, sir,' said Brad. 'That's why we'd need an order. You can see now that there is a second advantage for you in not obstructing us. And I can assure you, Lady Fortis, you will not be able to tell we worked in the grounds when we have finished.' There was a long silence; too long for Jim.

'Your choice,' he said. 'Arrest and exhumation versus a little quiet digging in your garden.'

There was a sudden flurry of movement. The library door banged.

'You have to be so uncouth?' asked Nicky, weakly.

'No, sir,' said Jim, unhelpfully.

'Do what you damned well like but don't upset Lady Fortis again!' He began to march up the stairs. Susie and I retreated into the study, closed the door. Nicky clattered past and on to his own room.

'We've a good view,' said Susie, returning to the window. I stood next to her, enjoyed her perfume. Reassuring her about the thunder last night had not led to anything else. But our quiet dinner and drinking in the bar, our separate sleeping on opposite sides of that damned wall, had all felt like promises. Arrogant sod I am. 'Here they come,' she said.

We watched the rainproofed crew get out of the van: Jim, Brad plus two other uniformed PCs. This appeared to be a signal for the drizzle to intensify. They valiantly ignored it and unloaded their equipment, which included two metal-detectors.

Their first problem was to locate the former position of the kennels and the area where the dogs had been shot down. The saturated grass strip obviously offered few clues. Maps were produced, sight lines were marked out, distances paced. These procedures were so boring to watch that Susie and I left the window and sat in armchairs to read. Not surprisingly, the warmth of the room made us drowsy, especially as our sleep had been so much disturbed by the violence of the rainstorm in the night. Slowly, Susie's eyes closed, her head turned to the left, her cheek brushed the leather of the chair wing. And I, instead of sleeping, sat and admired her beauty afresh, I could have drowned myself in her then, perhaps never to recover. (Marvellous fantasy!) But the occasional shout drifting through the drizzle and up to our window reminded me of matters other than lust and love.

We were dozing in the house where Hardwicke's accomplice or accomplices lived: accessories before, during and after the act. And *during* meant that the same charges could be brought as might have been brought against Hardwicke. Yet the sketchy evidence so far accumulated was barely sufficient to support a theory. It would not stand a chance in court. This made a second weakness even more significant: we had no idea of the motive for the setting up of Barnard Hardwicke as murderer.

It was a reasonable set of assumptions that he *had* committed murder, and by switching the dogs, and that *his* motive had been sexual — his desire for Lady Fortis. Subsequently, perhaps because he had panicked or because he realized Lady Fortis did not care for him, or for both reasons, he had killed himself. But why had he been set up in the first place?

The simple answer was that someone wanted Sir Gregory dead, didn't want their hands dirtied so set up the unfortunate lovesick vet. But what was the gain for that someone? We had no evidence at all that Lady Fortis needed the legacy of money and estate. She was rich from her first marriage. Similarly, Nicky Stapolous had benefited handsomely from his father's death. Neither of them were in debt. They lived well, at times extravagantly, almost wildly, but the occasional flings were making no significant impact on the vast assets they possessed.

The possibility that Lady Fortis or her son were involved in killings for any sick motive was also unlikely. Neither had been a witness of Sir Gregory's death, and Nicky's involvement in the death of the dogs could hardly be classified as sick enjoyment. And if Hardwicke's death was confirmed as suicide then presumably he died alone and not as a spectacle for a watching pervert.

And as for the attempted murder of PC Ashmore — well. My speculation that it was Nicky Stapolous who took the pot-shot at him rather than Barnard Hardwicke was merely a reasonable proposition based on what we knew about their respective personalities. I moved restlessly in my chair. Susie opened her eyes, smiled at me. I felt I would be unable to stand.

'How they doing?' she asked.

'Dunno.'

'I'll take a look.' She stood up, walked

to the window. I stayed in my seat and watched her. She began to shake with laughter. 'Come and see,' she said.

I staggered to her side. It was raining much harder now and the four disconsolate figures on the lawns below us were splashing half-heartedly over the grass. Markers had been put down, sweeps with the detectors were taking place, but they really needed a diving bell.

'On every flower a little rain must fall,' I said.

19

By late morning, frustrated by the rain and the water-logged soil, our colleagues had abandoned their search for bullets. Asserting separateness, Susie and I had stayed in the study for another hour. Apart from one of the domestic staff dusting the busts in the hall we had seen no one when we departed. At the Wheatsheaf Susie and I had lunch together, then retired to our separate rooms: she to write up reports for DCI Wilson, I to wrestle with a blocked poem. I made the mistake of lying down on the bed.

I was back in New York City walking with Lieutenant Al Newman. We were going to meet two Negro pushers who, according to Newman, wanted to sell out to us. I knew he had already sold me out. He believed my gun was in its shoulder holster beneath my overcoat buttoned to the neck against the blizzard. But I was holding it, catch off, in my overcoat pocket. 'Next left, Jack,' he whispered, brushing snow off his eyebrows.

The pushers were waiting for us forty yards down the alley. As we walked toward them they stepped apart offering two targets. Synchronized with their movements was Al's slowing of pace so that I walked ahead of him. At twenty yards I was in the middle of a triangle. At fifteen yards I was drawing, turning, firing two into his body, his gun discharging into the snow as he fell. The two Negros were still drawing their guns when I completed my turn and took them out as well. Neither got off a shot. I spun again to check on Newman, the most dangerous of the three, and looked directly into the double barrels of a shotgun. In the moment the triggers were pulled, the barrels flared, I realized the gun was held by a woman. But I had too little life left in me even to distinguish between Lady Fortis and Susie Green.

Eyes smarting from the brilliance of the flash, I pressed myself down on the bed to avoid the glare. Sunlight through my bedroom window was reflecting into my eyes from the dressing-table mirror. I rolled over face down into the pillow, hauled myself clear of the dream. Later, sitting in the armchair, I accepted that today's lunch might explain dreaming but not the subject of the dream. I don't know how long I sat there, but when Susie knocked on my door, letters in hand, I was ready to move.

'I'm driving over to Appleyard Hardy to post this stuff,' she said. 'Not risking the box here. Coming?' Successful only at dreaming I went with her.

'I'll make a round trip of it,' she said. 'We'll go out past Brad Ashmore's place; come back via Longbottom Lane. Never know who we'll meet.' Having no opinion I nodded, sat back, let her drive. Later, she switched on the car radio and we heard confirmation that the rainstorms of the last twenty-four hours had been the heaviest ever recorded in southern England.

'Hardly surprising everything's steaming in the sun,' said Susie.

'Be interesting to see what the ground's like around Swallows Wood having heard that story in the bar at lunch time.'

'You mean about its name, Jack?'

'Yes. I'd assumed it was named after the bird. Never thought of swallow *holes*. Of course, that explains the hummocky ground, the damp patches, the leaning trees in one part of the wood.'

'You think the storm was enough to flood the underground passages?'

'Likely, Susie. If they can't swallow all the rain there'll be surface water for the first time for years. The locals believe that heralds disaster.'

'We'll find out on the way back. Here's Ashmore's place. No sign of life. Maybe Mrs Ashmore's gone Saturday shopping while Jim and Brad are up at the Hardwicke place again. Just as well we're not seeing Jim. He's moaning about you, about having to work because you have hunches. When I last radioed him he kept asking for a fact or two.'

I didn't reply. How the hell did they all think *I* felt? I was operating the web of feelings that had yet to trap a fact. No one is thirstier for a fact than an intuitive.

At Appleyard Hardy, Susie parked

beside the green, got out, put her letters in the post box. I watched her walk back toward me. Mentally, I undressed her. Now *there* was a place where I'd've liked a few facts. She didn't open the car door but spoke through the open window.

'There's a little tea shop over there. How about Saturday afternoon tea?'

'Yes, please,' I said, leaping from the car. Alive again.

She slipped her arm through mine as we walked companionably round the green, both amused by the way the grass steamed in the afternoon heat. At the door of the tea shop she walked ahead of me. (Oh, that gorgeous bum!) She looked back over her shoulder and smiled. 'Shame about the others,' she said. 'But *we* have to stay in role. Archaeologists may have Saturday afternoons off.'

After the tea party she drove us slowly and sedately round the village, then out by the southern route that would take us back to Testem Magna via Longbottom Lane. As we approached the lane, as Swallows Wood began to bulk up on our left horizon, I began to feel edgy. I didn't say anything but knew Susie had picked up my nervousness, was watching me out of the corner of her eyes. As we rounded the bend we saw that the lane was under a sheet of water. Susie stopped the car. The flood was moving turgidly out of Swallows Wood at several different points. The water was orange-mud-brown, and carried a thick skin of dead leaves, twigs and ancient rubbish. 'We'll get through,' said Susie.

The water was only about six inches deep. As we rolled through it I wound down the window and listened to the water gurgling and lapping its way from the wood. It seemed to me the ground itself was bleeding onto the lane. The stench was appalling. I wound up the window.

'You never put that gate back,' said Susie. 'There it is against the hedge.' I scowled at it as we rolled past, daring another inanimate object to come to life. 'Well, well,' said Susie.

I jerked my head round to the front. Standing at the T junction, and clear of the flood waters, was a familiar figure leaning on his bicycle. Neatly, Susie brought us to a stop so that Brad Ashmore could speak to her without having to take a step.

'Thought you might be coming back this way, ma'am. A moment is required for conversation.'

'How did you know we'd gone?' I asked, a trifle uneasily.

'Saw you go past the house,' he said, wooden-faced.

'Didn't see you,' I said.

'In the bedroom with Debbie.' Unembarrassed, he smiled at us both. 'Then I checked with my colleague in Appleyard Hardy. Heard you were parked by the green, had gone into the tea shop. He phoned back when you left, telling me of your route.'

'You talk to the trees?' asked Susie, laughing.

'Haven't learned that one yet, ma'am.'

'And DS Douglas?' I said.

'Oh, out, Sergeant. Up at the kennels. One reason we were in the bedroom. We've been missing our — our privacy.'

'Yes,' said Susie, trying to sound severe.

'And what are you wanting to tell us?'

'At lunch time Nicky Stapolous telephoned me to report his motor bike stolen some time during the last week.'

'But I saw him working on it yesterday,' said Susie in astonishment.

'That was the smart machine, ma'am. He lost one of his two older bikes. He keeps 'em in one of the stables in the yard at the back of The Hall. Rarely gets 'em out now he's got the new superbike. Says that's why he can't be sure exactly when one was stolen. I told him to get down to the police house, my place, at once. Interesting, ma'am: he did not argue. Got there ten minutes later on the smart bike.

'As soon as he'd switched off the engine Detective Sergeant Douglas grabbed him, put him in his car and drove him up to the Hardwicke place. Nicky Stapolous identified the motor bike I had found in Hardwicke's barn.'

'And he sticks to the story it was nicked,' I asked.

'Unshakeable he is, Sergeant. DS Douglas drove him back to my place and we both had a go at him about it. But he stuck to his tale so we let him go home. Now I'm on my way to the Hardwicke place to get detailed statements from the staff.'

'Interesting day for you,' said Susie, naughtily. 'Any second thoughts?'

'Not yet, ma'am. I'm not sure that *how* Hardwicke obtained use of that bike is much of a significance. What interests me more at the moment is that Nicky Stapolous asked us no questions. DS Douglas said he was also silent up at the kennels. Perhaps he already knows answers. Makes me wonder how secure the boy feels.'

'Or he knows he's lost,' I said. Brad stirred uneasily, adjusted the position of his bicycle.

'*We* don't *know* that,' he said. 'That'd be a hard thing to decide. Meanwhile, ma'am and Sergeant, I must go up to the kennels. If we don't have more rain DS Douglas and I intend to be back in the metal-detecting business tomorrow. Good day.' He stepped away from the car, did a slow-motion vault onto his bicycle, rode away toward Hardwicke's place.

'I think that how Hardwicke obtained use of that bike is very significant,' I said.

'So do I,' said Susie.

We watched Brad until he disappeared round the curve in the lane. Behind us water gurgled and sighed in Swallows Wood.

20

By evening opening time, cloudless May was re-established, so we took our drinks into the garden. Only near-tropical humidity reminded us of the great storms of the past twenty-four hours. I followed Susie to the table she chose and sat facing her. Then I realized I could see that damned stone leering at me round the corner of the hotel. I wiped my handkerchief over my forehead.

'Just as well the weather's changed so much,' she said. 'It seems a great deal of damage has been done. The sooner the ground dries out the better. I overheard two men talking in the bar while you were ordering. They said that every ditch and culvert is full for miles around. Not surprising Swallows Wood is temporarily unable to take all that water.'

I did not reply. I had recognized the very large black car creeping to the front of the Wheatsheaf. Susie looked over her shoulder to find out what had distracted me. I heard her draw a deep breath. We watched as James brought the car to a smooth halt. Dressed in his familiar butling black, he stepped down, held open the rear door for Lady Fortis. Dressed entirely in white, and carrying a white handbag, she paused, smoothed her dress, said something to James. He got back into the car and drove away. She turned toward the hotel, saw us sitting in the garden, hesitated, then walked in through the front door.

'It could be we're getting company,' I said.

'And just after her son's been grilled by Jim,' said Susie. 'Could mean we've been rumbled.'

If I say that Isobel Fortis entered the garden like a determined sleep-walker that may give some idea of how she was, but I doubt if words exist to describe her manner. Analogy was with the victim of an execution I attended in South Africa. He had drifted rather than walked to the scaffold; perhaps part of his mind anaesthetized by disbelief. He had only

216

come to full consciousness when the noose first touched his skin. That was when I understood that the hood was placed over the victim's head not to spare him anything but to protect the spectators from the expression on his face. Being her executioners, we did the polite thing and stood.

'May I join you for a few minutes?' she asked, nervously, one hand smoothing the waist of her dress. We made certain sociable noises. She sat down next to Susie and facing me.

The symbolic and the real became fused in that moment as I faced the Testing Stone, Susie and Isobel. The solid, tawny mass of stone; the voluptuous sun-fired blonde dressed in boldly patterned gold flowers on a green field; the dark, slim, lissom white-dressed girl-woman awaiting the noose. An enormous emotional weight held me in my seat. No possibility of offering to fetch her a drink. My head seemed to be filled by a loud noise, as of violent rain upon a rock.

Then she caused the fawning landlord

to materialize beside her, three drinks on his tray.

'I hope you will forgive me for presuming to reorder for you,' she said. 'But Mr Wentall was able to tell me your previous order.'

We stuttered denials of enmity. Mr Wentall placed the drinks, then grovelled his way across the lawn and back into his hotel.

'Your good health,' she said, solemnly, raising a spirit glass full of a colourless liquid. We responded to the toast. She shuddered over her drink, hastily put down the glass.

'We have not seen you here before, Lady Fortis,' said Susie. Thank Christ one of us at the table was functioning normally.

'Never been here before,' she said. With a visible effort she made herself drink again. She put her glass down on the table. The three of us looked at the pool of spilt drink curving itself round a protuberance in the oiled wood. Then she began to talk rather fast.

'I decided to bring Nicky in by car. He

218

was much too upset to be allowed to ride his motor bike again today. That wretched village policeman had about as much tact as . . . Not content with getting Nicky to identify a stolen motor bike he now wants a written statement as well. The man's a fool.'

'Police routine, I suppose,' I said, inanely.

'Worse than that. He then said that he would like my son formally to identify Barnard Hardwicke, that unfortunate vet who killed himself the other day. You have heard about that? I'm sure you have. It must be the talk of the village. People here prefer gossip to bread. That idiot policeman requires identification both by an employee and some other person. Apparently, there's no family, no relative. It seems grossly unfair that Nicky be dragged into something so distasteful merely because of the unfortunate coincidence that it happened to be *his* old bike that was stolen and then dumped up at the kennels.'

Susie and I looked at each other. Our colleagues were building the pressure.

'I simply couldn't let him come in again on that new bike of his, so I got James to drive us both in. We left Nicky at the police house or station, whatever it is, and I came on here. The dear boy was adamant I should not wait there. He is determined I should not in any way become involved.' She took another sip of the disliked drink. The Testing Stone continued to watch us. 'I have sent James back to fetch him and then we will all go home.'

'And the identification of the body?' I asked.

'Certainly not. I made it quite clear on the telephone that if that policeman tries to insist on Nicky doing something others are equally competent to do I will telephone the Chief Constable. The whole business is a nonsense. After all, that unfortunate man must have a solicitor and accountant. Let one of them do it.' Her voice wavered slightly but raised no protective feelings in me. It was possible that 'unfortunate man' had murdered for her, and that 'that idiot policeman' had lived through two months and more of hell.

'Lady Fortis, perhaps the police have a particular reason for wanting your son to help.'

She stared at me, surprised by my dislike as much as by my words. She was not used to dislike being allowed to surface. So remarkable a response to her person almost drowned the meaning of the words. Then she recovered.

'What can you possibly mean by that, Dr Bull?'

'He was able and willing to help with the identification of your late husband when, as I understand it, there was not much left to identify.'

The grey pallor in her cheeks became more pronounced. I wondered if she was going to faint. Not she. 'That remark is really quite . . . They — they checked the dental records as well.'

Bet they did, I thought. Just in case it was a switch and the Reds had made off with the real Sir Gregory. 'Well, Lady Fortis, perhaps the police were impressed by the way your son coped in that difficult situation, so they thought of him for this identification. Especially as Mr Hardwicke was a great friend of yours.'

She turned her face toward Susie as if seeking an ally, as if reminding her of their long, superficially inconsequential conversation in the library two days earlier. Susie responded by not meeting her eyes, by casually raising and draining her glass.

'He *was* a great friend of yours?' I persisted.

'Not of *mine*, Dr Bull. A friend of my husband's. And that was based only on common interests in dogs and shooting.'

'Shooting?'

'Mr Hardwicke was a shooting guest of my husband's on the estate. The two of them and Nicky often went out together.'

'I think some of your villagers have romantic notions,' said Susie, innocently smiling. Momentarily, Lady Fortis's dark eyes appeared to gleam with hope. Here was escape by taking offence. But she was defeated by the realization her car had not yet returned and by my overbearing insistence on buying her another drink. I marched into the bar but took my time reordering. Nothing was lost by leaving my bright lady with my dark.

I stood in the doorway with my tray of drinks and looked out on my ladies. Why was it the dark one reminded me of all the women I had ever had, but the blonde made me forget them? As I walked stealthily toward them over the drying damp grass I saw how rigidly Isobel Fortis held herself together: back straight, elbows in sides, rounded calves in their white stockings squeezed together under the bench. Susie had just concluded a typists'-pool remark about 'third time lucky'.

'I have absolutely no time for such vulgar gossip! Thank you,' she added as I placed her drink in front of her. Vodka, Mr Wentall had said. As I sat down again the great black car glided to a halt in front of the Wheatsheaf. No one got out. I wondered if there was some way we could hold her there just a little longer. Then Nicky Stapolous wound down the rear window, stuck his head out.

'Come!' he commanded.

That harsh, croaked order made her jump, blush like a girl. She drained her glass in one gesture. 'Come,' he had said; not 'Mother' but 'Come.'

Seeing his mother raise the glass he must have assumed she had not heard him. But he did not call again. Instead, he jabbed one finger in her direction, said something to James who swung down from the car and began to amble toward the side gate of the garden. But Lady Fortis was already moving.

'I must go,' she said, cold again, the staining blush gone from her white face.

We all stood up and, in the process of raising my left leg over the bench, I turned to the left facing directly toward the Testing Stone. In one swift arching downward sweep it fell. The lawn twitched under us like a beaten rug, apple tree boughs groaned, tiles began to skitter hysterically down the catslide roof of the hotel. As the ground reverberated like a toneless bell a great cloud of spray rose lingeringly out of the bruised earth round the fallen Testing Stone.

'On, no!' My own shock and the appalling noise of the stone falling could not deafen me to that whisper of agony.

Turning, I saw Lady Isobel in a dishevelled heap on the ground. Before either Susie or I could move, James Webb had swooped, gathered, raised his unconscious mistress. For one majestic moment he confronted us, his face almost black above the white form he held. Her head rested against his left breast, her legs hung over his right arm, while her left arm, which he had somehow failed to gather cleanly, hung down like the neck of a dead swan.

The world began to close in: Nicky's voice petulant from the car demanding explanations, people running from the hotel, Susie grasping my arm as she stepped round the table to join me. But I watched James Webb as he turned away, walked away in slow grandeur with his burden. I felt ashamed I had ever perceived him as a comical figure.

21

The falling of the stone did not mark the end of its power either for me or for the village. It dominated the Saturday night dinner conversations in the Wheatsheaf, where a gloomy-faced Mr Wentall supervised his staff. Standing by our table, he expressed the opinion the stone would never be raised. He brightened a little at my malicious suggestion of a commemorative plaque describing the event and attributing it to the effects of the Great May Rainstorm. He also pondered my personal usefulness as the archaeologist in residence at the time. But these slender advertising advantages could not combat his depression at loss of erection. Instead of an impressive stone beacon marking his hotel he now had an extremely large but low-lying slab, its future role merely a climbing block for young children while their parents enjoyed a drink in the garden.

'Suppose it be something it didn't break,' he said, turning away to fetch the sweet trolley for Susie.

'Ironic, isn't it?' she said. 'The saturation of very dry ground that caused the fall is probably also the reason it didn't shatter.'

'Very logical,' I said, sourly. She looked at me but said nothing until Mr Wentall had served her and wheeled the trolley away.

'So what are you making of it? The same as Lady Fortis perhaps?'

'Dunno,' I said. 'She'd obviously got hold of some local superstition and insinuated it into her life. But apparently she soon recovered. Couldn't come to the phone when I rang The Hall to check but the maid said she was resting before coming down to dinner.'

'So, Jack, you believe it marks a disaster for her. You may be right the way the case is going. In fact she'd probably picked up some signals about that at the unconscious level long before the stone fell. Perhaps the fall was merely confirmation for her.'

'Very likely. How about my question?'

'Try me.'

'Why did it fall down *then*, Susie?'

She did not answer for several minutes but concentrated on her food. I drank the last of my wine. Eventually, she looked across the table at me, the candlelight twisting the shadows of her face.

'Jack, I've seen you take some pretty accurate and incisive leaps of intuition. My experience of you helps me to understand why Frimmer took you on. *My* mental block is about wish-fulfilment.'

'You mean I may choose to want to make an event more significant than it is?'

'I'm glad you understand, Jack. I didn't want you to think — '

'Don't worry, Susie. I understand. Also I happen to think you are right. I have to keep checking and rechecking where I am with all this intuition business, and with wishing to convince myself something has a kind of magic it doesn't really possess. Fortunately, it's not entirely up to me to do the checking.'

'What do you mean?'

'That life itself offers up checks and balances, just as it offers up crises, disasters, blessings. So what I have to do is wait and see. Something will tell me either that my imagination is getting overheated or that imagination has nothing to do with it. No need for me to press. After all, the thing about the bullets and the dogs came to me because I left the idea alone for a time.'

'You sound so clear about it, Jack.'

'Don't be taken in, Susie.' I couldn't help laughing. 'I'm talking clearly only about *experiencing* the processes. The processes themselves baffle me as much as anyone else — including Jung. Sometimes I doubt if intuition actually exists, so often it could be some clever combination of quick, accurate reasoning plus a clever guess or two.'

'Liar,' she said. 'And that's not my intuition working. Just knowing a devil's advocate when I meet one!'

I leaned across the table, took hold of her right hand and kissed it.

'Jack! You're supposed to be a respectable archaeologist.'

'But not desexed, ma'am. Shall I order coffee?'

'Please,' she said. Then, before I could summon the waitress: 'There's another question, Jack.'

'Yes?' I said, already knowing.

'Why, out of all the village, did she come to sit with *us*.'

'I feel she already knows why we are here in Testem Magna.'

Much later, sitting in the bar, she made some remark about taking a short walk if the evening was still fine. Leaning back across the settle I pulled the curtain aside. I heard her quick indrawn breath. Testem Magna had vanished.

'Not quite walking weather,' I said.

Heavy mist draped over the valley, pressed on the windows of the Wheatsheaf. All that rain was beginning to return to the sky, drawn up by afternoon warmth and now chilled by the night. Inwardly, I shivered at thoughts of what it must now be like in Swallows Wood. The last of the surface water would be subsiding back into the swallow holes. The mist would be edging and sidling between the trees, dampening the barks, forming droplets on the end of the smaller branches. There would be distracting, hateful noises echoing moistly between the trunks. And there would be the stench of damp decay.

'No evening walk,' I said. 'Let's go upstairs and chew the fat.' Surprised by her silence, I looked closely into her face. Her eyes were wet.

'Susie,' I said, touching her thigh. 'What is it, my dear?'

'*That*'s what it is,' she said, impatiently. 'You calling me that. And kissing my hand. We simply cannot, dare not, make *that* mistake. You know how I feel about it. I explained when we first started on this case.'

'Yes,' I said. Then I was struck dumb by happiness. I nodded my head at her.

She took my hand from her thigh, gently transferred it to the seat between us. 'You understand me, believe my reasons?' I nodded again. 'When we've finished these drinks I'll come with you to your room but to work. You can help me write the next stage of the daily record for DCI Wilson: a no-nonsense report. I do not think that dour gentleman wishes to know that the Testing Stone has fallen down.'

So we did it. And it was pleasant enough: two highly trained professionals agreeing a report. But how hard to work with her so close, and close in so many ways. I managed it — of course. But for most of the time I lay well back in the armchair, avoided looking directly at her stretched out on my bed. And when she stood up to go back to her room I remained in the chair, just reached up and touched the hand she momentarily rested on my shoulder. Our good-nights drifted soft like the mist.

So I found myself alone and womanless in a hotel bedroom at 10 p.m. on a Saturday night, having no wish to get on with the current poem, finding my small cache of paperbacks unappealing. I wandered aimlessly round the room, looked out into the mist, unable to see even as far as the recumbent stone. I undressed, lay on the bed, a book unopened on my chest. I stared at the ceiling for a long time. Then they came to me out of the mist.

First, I heard again, the chilling, flat, thumping blow of the Testing Stone falling; then saw again the black-visaged, black-clad man holding the woman in white in his arms. I could almost feel that passionate yet sexless devotion he had for her. Caliban he might be but she would come to no harm with him.

The harm had come from another.

I am physically present but invisible. She, Lady Fortis, lying in bed at dawn; early morning light illuminating the room through white blinds. A knock on the door. A young, pyjama'd Nicky Stapolous comes in. She opens her arms, murmurs: 'Happy Birthday, darling.' He does not immediately enter that embrace but stands staring down at his mother. Then thickly, as if choking, he speaks.

'Now I am sixteen one law has gone.'

A convulsive shudder runs through the woman, her arms fall to the bed as if her cortex has been severed. She makes an attempt to speak, forming the words: 'You fool', but fails to utter them. Then he swoops over her, throws back the covers, slides arrogantly, possessively into the bed, drags the covers back over them both. Whatever protest she speaks it is not strong enough to reach me through the covers, through his embrace. Then it is not words she utters.

I stared at the ceiling of my hotel room, at the pattern of light and dark cast across the woodchip paper; a surface like a child's dream of the moon.

All we had ever lacked was motive.

Later, I reset my alarm for 5.30 a.m.

22

Wise choice of hour: enough light but concealment in the mist. I put out my right hand and gently rubbed the nearest corner of the Testing Stone. It was slippery with dew. There was one more thing the stone could do for me. I bent down, put two logs on the ground and against the stone. Then I stepped back, drew my pistol. Taking very careful aim I fired two shots into the logs. Sounds of gunshots, splintering of the logs, impacting of part-spent bullets into the stone, were carried away into the mist. Hastily, I sorted through the splinters and split logs at the face of the stone. I could only find one bullet but one was all I needed. Retarded by the wood, deformed by impact on the stone, it resembled a bullet enough to convince someone who knew a lot about guns. A star-shaped blemish on the stone would not be identifiable at all. I tossed the larger fragments of the logs back into Wentall's fuel shed. I went back into the hotel, relocked the outer door, ran up to my room.

She had recognized the sounds even as they had woken her, now stood in the doorway of her room, one hand in her dressing-gown pocket. As she opened her mouth I raised a finger to my lips. Then I led her back into her room, made her sit on the bed next to me. Then I was ready to speak.

'Look,' I said, showing her the battered bullet.

'Why?'

'Jim Douglas must find a bullet,' I said. 'I'm making sure he does so.'

'What has happened?' She rubbed her wrist where I had held her.

So I told her. Her eyes changed their shape a little. All she said was: 'So that could be the wound.' Later she said: 'How could she bear it? How could she?' She expected no answer; received none. After another long pause she sighed, then said: 'You must go back to your room. I'll try to talk more of this later.'

'Right,' I said. 'In about an hour I'm

taking a brisk walk round the back of the village and out to Ashmore's cottage. All I shall tell Jim is that we want him to pretend to find this bullet. No need to talk of dreams.' As I opened the door and stepped out of her room I heard her whisper: 'Poor woman, poor woman!'

Half an hour later I radioed Jim and set up a meet for 6.45 a.m. in the copse behind Ashmore's house. When it was time I walked out of the village and along the lane toward Ashmore's place. The mist distorted object and distance, created the illusion I was dreaming the event. Other dream images slid tentatively across the screen of my mind. I rejected them, concentrated on the walk, on the possibility of missing the track to the copse.

Jim was leaning against a tree, hands in pockets of his raincoat. We had met in a wood before now. As I walked up to him my footsteps were an echo of water dripping from the trees.

'Right time to start work on a Sunday,' he said, irritably.

'Less likely to be seen,' I said, equally

irritable. 'Here, you have to find this in the lawn this morning.'

He took the deformed bullet from the palm of my hand, stared at it, then at me.

'Evidence?' he said, non-committal.

'No. It'd never get past a defence expert as being an Armalite round. It's simply to prod the Fortis family into more action.'

'It'll do that thing, will it, Jack?'

'Hope so.' (He would hear nothing of dreams or fantasies from me.)

'A fact would be nice, even a little one,' he said, almost wistfully. 'A diet of your crappy hunches and theories gets a bit indigestible.'

'Tough titty,' I said. 'But we've got two deaths and an attempted murder to soothe your savage.'

'OK, OK,' said Jim, wearily. 'Maybe this little trophy will encourage some bugger to sing a bit.' With a disgusted expression on his face he passed the misshapen lump of lead from hand to hand, then put it in his pocket. 'Tell Ashmore?'

'No,' I said. 'Let him and his mates

think it's kosher. That'll lead 'em to behave convincingly when we try to nail that Nicky Stapolous.'

'Ah,' said Jim. 'He *is* your front runner then?'

'If I said 'yes' to that you'd only write it off as another crazy hunch.'

'Never ever said *crazy*,' snapped Jim. 'If I thought *that* I'd long ago've asked Frimmer to ditch you. Mind you, if this don't work — '

'All we've got!' I turned away and crashed out of the copse. His forbearance was even more infuriating than his scepticism.

At 8.45 a.m. I knocked on Susie's door, went in when she called. She was dressed and ready to go down for breakfast.

'All right?' she asked.

'Yes.'

'Replacements,' she said, handing me two bullets. I looked down at them lying new and shiny in my left palm. Perhaps I resembled Jim Douglas at that moment. But he knew the destination of that spent bullet. I had no idea where my two would come to rest: spent, deformed. Hastily, I transferred them to my pocket.

At breakfast, Susie did most of the talking. She effectively demolished the whole of my theory about the case, then, just as effectively, reassembled it in the most positive terms. Rather more gently, she spoke of the insufficiency of evidence. (No point in telling her Jim had already underlined.) If Barnard Hardwicke had indeed murdered Sir Gregory by changing the dogs who was able to *confirm* that? If the motive was obsession with Lady Fortis who would confirm that? And if it was true that Barnard Hardwicke had been encouraged in his mad scheme by Nicky Stapolous would Nicky Stapolous ever confirm that? And as for Nicky's dark motive in seeking his stepfather's death, and as for his mother's support — active or passive — would either of them ever be persuaded to enter my wakeful dream and confess it true?

'Their staff?' I said, feebly.

'Frequently changed and working in so large a house? Interconnecting bedrooms? Someone as devoted as James Webb?'

240

I had nothing else to say.

We left the Wheatsheaf at 9.45 a.m. The mist still choked the valley but the light was changing. One could almost feel the sunlight burning away the top of the mist, thinning it, dispersing it.

'You drive,' said Susie.

As we approached the gatehouse of The Hall I became aware of another vehicle travelling behind us in the mist and closing. I told Susie. She turned and watched.

'Damn!' she said. 'It's a van. Could be Jim's party. We don't want to arrive in convoy. We've still some use for our cover. Drive on past the gates, Sergeant.'

I did so, and saw in my mirror that the van had turned into the drive. 'How long?' I asked.

'Give them ten minutes. Long enough to rouse people at The Hall and let them know they've come back again to work over the same ground.'

Parked in a field entrance we waited ten minutes, watched the mist thinning down until visibility was almost a hundred yards. Minutes so much like that early morning at the Steel stones and our first gropings into another kind of mist. No suspicion then of what it concealed. Yet it had always been a simple case — if only we had been able to see. High song of a lark confirmed that sunlight was overhead. 'Let's move,' said Susie.

As we rolled along the long tarmac drive the mist rolled ahead of us. We could see the nearest fields, mysterious shapes of cows. Then, when about four hundred yards away, The Hall began to climb through the mist: sunlit roofs and domes rising rootless, unsupported in the morning light. Castle Dread. At three hundred yards the whole building was revealed: roofs now tied to walls, and they to the earth. At two hundred yards I selected neutral, switched off, kept the clutch down. We rolled silently except for the susurrus of tyres on tarmac. Somewhere away to our left voices could be heard as the other part of our team made their way toward the grassed killing ground.

'Back or front?' I said.

'Front this time,' she said. 'The others

can cover the back of the house.'

The Range Rover crept quietly up the gravelled slope. I parked behind the terrace wall just before we reached the great flight of steps. We were not visible from the house. I pulled on the handbrake. Summer sounds as the last mist was drawn away. We looked into each other's faces for a moment.

'Take care,' she said. Then: 'Let's go!'

I stepped down onto the gravel, locked the car door, eased the position of my pistol in my long thigh pocket. I walked round the front of the car and stood next to Susie. Then together we began to walk up the great flight of steps. Halfway up, just before we came into line of sight of the first floor windows of The Hall, the great fountain sprang into life behind us. Turning startled, we watched for a moment as the jet rose, swayed, steadied, settled to a cascade of summer light.

23

The housemaid who opened the door was surprised to see us. I explained that Lady Fortis had invited us to work in Sir Gregory's study whenever we wished.

'But being Sunday, sir, her ladyship is at church.'

'That's all right,' said Susie. 'We've been coming here most of the week without Lady Fortis wanting to meet us every time.'

'Yes, ma'am, I'm sure. But Mr Stapolous is out as well. He's gone shooting over by Downham Wood. I told the policemen that as well. If you wouldn't mind . . . ' Footsteps on the first floor landing echoed behind and above her. We looked up. James Webb came into view, descended the stairs. It felt like a long time for him to reach the hall floor. The housemaid stepped toward him, began to speak, stopped as he raised his right hand.

'They come,' he articulated. That he spoke clearly somehow crystallized the agonizing sense of tension that possessed the house.

'Thank you, James,' said Susie, gravely. 'We wish to work in the study until lunch time.'

Equally gravely, he inclined his head, walked round us, closed the door behind us. We were closed in with him in the mausoleum. The housemaid scuttled away and disappeared through the archway under the stairs. I didn't like that at all, the scuttling, I mean. I stepped a pace away from Susie but no one opened fire. As we climbed the stairs we looked back and down at James Webb. He was standing perfectly still in front of the door, arms by his sides, head tilted, watching our ascent. I turned away from his stare, sure he understood our link with the policemen digging in the grounds. I was not alone in passing from the stages of suspicions, guesses and dreams.

In the study, Susie organized our morning into half-hour shifts taking turns to keep watch at the window. We would need to know at once when Jim Douglas decided to 'find' the bullet I had given him. We might not be able to use our radios. Susie had first watch, I went back to reading Thom on stone circles. Not really reading at all, but possessed by the house, by its witnessing, its waiting. Events had turned mortar to dust; the stones in the walls seemed to slide on each other in fear. A pretentious, ornate but solid house had become a house of cards. One further blow would topple it — and we would be crushed in the ruin.

About twenty minutes into that first session, Susie turned away from the window and beckoned me. I joined her, looked out and down across the grounds. We could see the entrance to the stable yard just below us and to our left. A white Porsche was being driven in. We watched Lady Fortis, who was wearing a red coat and a black hat, park the car, climb out, lock the door. This took place in the one corner of the yard that was cut off from Jim's line of sight.

'Jim couldn't be sure it was her,' I said.

'More likely he's saving the bullet for Nicky's return,' said Susie. 'You take over here, Jack. I'll wander to the loo, see if I can check on Lady Fortis's location in the house. Just wait a minute.' She walked to the door, opened it about six inches. We heard Lady Fortis come into the hall from the back of the house, speak to the maid. The maid began to climb the stairs. Susie shut the door.

'I think she has gone into the library,' she whispered. 'The maid's bringing her coat and hat up to the bedroom. Once she's out of the way I'll prowl round.'

When she left me I stood at the window and watched our colleagues working. As the two PCs completed each sweep with the metal-detectors Jim and Brad moved the marker tapes to new positions. Then they marked their charts, made a visual inspection of the next strip of ground. Jim was playing it straight despite the bullet burning his pocket. Ironic if he did find a bullet. He could use it in exactly the same way and it *would* be evidence in court.

'Still at it?' asked Susie when she

returned. She came and stood beside me. 'Be funny if they found a genuine bullet as well.'

'That's what I was thinking. Lady Fortis?'

'Settled in the library. Just had coffee taken in. I suppose she'll read the Sunday papers until Nicky gets back for lunch.'

'Or sit staring at the wall,' I said. Susie looked at me, nodded.

'You can feel it everywhere in the house,' she said. 'A tension, a waiting. And I can tell you what that feeling is, Jack. It's just like Friday afternoon before it rained: feeling of imminent change, something dramatic is about to happen. And just this once I'm quite sure the feeling is outside of me, is not something I'm creating and then putting out onto someone or something else.'

'With you, Susie,' I said, touching her left wrist with my fingertips. 'We just have to stay quiet, keep our minds clear. Meanwhile, Jim digs.'

'Yes, Jack. That's how it's got to be. Will you stay on watch for a while? I'll take over the next half hour.'

So I kept watch while she pretended to read. Then we changed places, then changed again. Description of what we did does not convey the confused sensations created by the passage of time. I was for ever checking my watch. In each thirty minute period time did not pass at all for the first twenty-five minutes. Then all the clocks jumped the full half hour. We changed places almost at a run. I noticed Susie surreptitiously winding her watch when she thought I wasn't looking.

I had been back at the window for the third time for about fifteen minutes when Jim Douglas started gesticulating at his helpers, holding out one hand as they closed on him.

'Susie!' I said. She was beside me at once.

'Why now?' she asked.

I did not have to reply. Nicky Stapolous came into view walking close to the house and toward the stable yard. He was carrying a very short-barrelled shotgun under his arm, a bulging game bag over his shoulder. As he walked his attention was focused entirely on the pantomime performance organized by Jim. Then he began to walk much more quickly. Susie took her radio from her bag, switched on. We saw Jim raise his set.

'Sergeant,' she said. 'Your men cover the back. Jack'll take the front. Move your men up now. Then you meet me in the library. Out.'

'Jack, you get out front. Nicky'll be out of all our views in a moment. He could run through the house and get away. I'm for the library. Move it!'

We hurtled down that curving staircase. No caution or finesse if our bluff was to work. The noise we made must have reached the staff quarters. It certainly preceded us to the entrance hall and the library. As Susie and I took our different routes from the bottom of the staircase Lady Fortis, dressed all in black, opened the library door, made to step out into the hall.

'Stay in there!' ordered Susie, making no attempt to hide the radio she was carrying. As she hustled Lady Fortis back into the library, and I ran on to the front door, I caught the briefest glimpse of

Lady Fortis's face changing colour.

I ran across the terrace, down the great flight of steps, stopped beside the Range Rover. Listened. Only the fountain. I checked that all the car doors were locked. Then I leaned against the bonnet, drew my pistol, checked, snapped off safety. And while I did that the lovely summer morning surrounded me, the splashing, glittering fountain seductively poured itself out almost at my feet.

When I heard the metallic click of the shotgun snapping shut I realized how completely I had been seduced. He had not come down the stairs after all. The fountain had drowned out all sound of his footsteps in the gravel as he came round the end of the house and terrace.

'Stand quite still,' said Nicky, softly. 'You move and you're dead.'

24

He came at me from my right, from behind the Range Rover. I was facing the fountain. Not hearing him was my mistake; approaching from my right was his. Being left-handed I had the gun in my left, down at my thigh. He couldn't see it. But the double-barrelled shotgun was pointing at my throat from fifteen feet away. Despite the short barrels, the cone of buckshot would scarcely have spread by the time it struck me. In the instant we stood staring I recollected Frimmer's request: an arrest rather than a corpse. I kept the pistol pressed against my thigh.

'What the hell — ' I said.

'Don't even bother,' he said. 'We're not totally silly. We've been wondering about you and your lady friend.'

'But what do you — '

'*I said don't bother*!' As he paused I recognized in his voice what the tragic affair was for him: will-to-power gone bad. And mad? I kept silent. 'Yes,' he said. 'Even if you're not the law you're still in my way. I'd love to blow your head off.'

I believed him. I stood absolutely still apart from the heaving of my chest, the faint flutter in the back of my knees.

'Keys for this vehicle?'

Allowing myself to look both bewildered and frightened, I half-turned away from him, slipped the pistol, safety still off, into my trouser pocket. The gamble was on his ignorance that I was armed. I fussed in both pockets pretending to search for keys.

'No,' I said. 'She's got them. My assistant's got them.' I leaned against the car bonnet. I thought that denial was the bravest thing I'd ever done; I still do.

Nicky continued to stare at me, his eyes blacker, deeper. 'Could be,' he said, at last. 'Now get away from the car! I can still start it without keys. Back off!'

I stepped away, away from the car, away from the steps, turning, edging back toward the fountain. I stopped when my left heel slammed against the low circular wall that held the pond. I felt a fine brush of spray across the back of my neck, damping down the bristling short hairs. Hands at my sides where Nicky could see them, I waited for him to break into the Range Rover. Then he spoke again, his voice raised against the continuous splashing of the water beside me.

'In a moment James will bring Lady Fortis here. Told James where I would be as I dodged through the house. She'll come with me. He'll look after you. Make no trouble and you'll come to no harm. Understand?'

I nodded. His announcement per-suaded me not to shoot him just yet; wait until mother and servant arrived. Never will I understand why I believed that James Webb and Isobel Fortis might outwit Susie and four other police officers. But I knew it was vital to wait. So I let him take his eyes off me for a moment while he smashed the car window with his gun butt. I just put my hands in my pockets, hunched my shoulders in distress and terror at this vandalism. Triumphantly, he opened the door, stepped away from the car.

'Now we wait,' he said. 'I'll by-pass ignition once James is here to watch you.' He also assumed my colleagues would be outwitted. Was there still something about his mother I did not know; something I had not anticipated, that was even now to defeat us? Or was it his madness speaking? I felt slightly sick.

Nicky took several paces to his left so the glittering cascade of the sunlit fountain was not directly in his line of sight. Now he stood facing me, gun pointing at my chest. We were ten yards apart. Behind him, the flight of stone steps climbed to the terrace; beyond that, over his head, I could see the roofs of The Hall. Behind me and to my left, the circular pond of the fountain lay behind the curved stone wall that stood twelve inches above the gravel of the path. I hoped the water was very deep otherwise that twelve inches of stonework would be the total height of my protection when we started shooting. I got both things wrong: depth of water, and the assumption that we would fire the first shots.

There was shouting in the house. I braced myself. Determinedly, Nicky kept his face toward me, not looking back up the steps. Much louder shouting and clear separation of voices suggested that people were spilling out of the front door. Still he held steady, probably supported by the belief James and his mother were escaping toward him. Then a single shot from The Hall was too much for Nicky.

Jaw dropping, he began to turn his head, to look back over his shoulder. In slow motion (that was how it *felt*!) I began to draw my pistol. Realization came to Nicky. As he reversed the movement of his head, tightened his finger on the trigger, I hurled myself sideways into the pond, tried to dive into the shelter of the retaining wall. In the moment of splitting my skull on the concrete floor under three inches of water, the edge of the shotgun blast fanned agonizingly across my right hip and thigh, and my first shot hit Nicky in the chest.

As I clawed my way up against the edge of the pond, blood already spurting from above my left ear and eye, Nicky began to fall back toward the steps, his head turning tiredly to his left, the shotgun sagging toward the ground. My second shot caught him in the face and because his head was sideways on to me that one shot blew out both eyes. The body slammed back and down on to the steps, propped in a half-sitting posture. The shotgun clattered into the gravel but the second barrel did not discharge.

Next I knew I was lying on my back in the water, the fountain spray mixing with the blood coming out of my head. And I had lost my pistol somewhere in the pond. I don't think I lost consciousness despite the terrible blow. What I did lose was awareness of the minor wound in my side; insignificant compared with the agony in my head. Then I heard someone coming down the stone steps.

I turned on my right side in the water, clawed at the edge of the pool, raised my head. It was Lady Fortis. She was running down the steps toward Nicky's seated corpse. As I scrabbled at the pool edge, raised myself to a kneeling position, I heard her saying: 'No, no, no, no,' repeated on a flat dulled note. She saw me and that shotgun in the instant when I knew I couldn't get to it first. Desperately, I raked at the shallow, reddening water with both hands, in vain hope of finding my pistol. Then I stopped moving. She was bending, picking up the shotgun. At ten yards the blast was going to rip my shattered head off my shoulders.

Something was said by one of us. Not sure who spoke, did not hear the words. She moved back, sat on the bottom step next to the corpse of her lover and son, raised the gun until the short barrels pointed into my face. She continued to raise the barrels. By the time she was aiming at the top of the fountain column I knew her target. But my injuries, or my compassion, prevented me dragging myself clear of the pond and across the gravel. Finally, when she had twisted, lowered and positioned the gun with the barrel muzzles under her chin she pulled the triggers. She could only have done it with her son's gun.

As the steps behind her changed

colour, figures came into view at the top of the flight on the terrace edge. They stood quite still. To my left someone came round the corner, stood next to the car, was violently sick. As I began to slide back into the water I turned my head, caught a glimpse of Brad Ashmore bowed forward, shoulders heaving. I slipped down behind the little wall, began to drown in inches of water under the sweetly playing fountain.

25

Callously, Jim Douglas ripped the skin from my last banana, bit its head off.

'Pleasure to see you tidied up and in what passes for your right mind,' he said. 'I hear your side was only a bit skinned and your head has been stitched up.'

'Yes,' I said, curtly. I was fed up with my hospital bed, my head was still sore and I had been looking forward to eating that banana. I was not at all sorry about his black eye.

'Done yourself a bitta good,' Jim said. 'Lying here in a private room for five days while the rest of us had to do the sorting. Not that we could sort that much. Lady Fortis gave absolutely nothing away before James Webb started the fight in the library.'

'So Frimmer told me.'

'Oh, the great man's visited, has he?'

'His banana,' I lied, maliciously. I need not have bothered. Jim gulped down its tail without blanching. 'Honoured, wasn't I?' I said.

'Don't lay too much store on one visit, mate. He's pretty bloody peeved that once again you've not made an arrest.'

'So I gather. Tough titty. But we've got James Webb.'

'Can't do him for much other than assaulting, impeding etc. He did his best to help Lady Fortis get away.'

'Caught you a nice one in the process.'

'Unexpectedness of it. He was just standing in the doorway scowling, then bang! Something Lady Fortis said activated his mainspring. After he'd hit me he tossed PC Ashmore and his two colleagues around the room. Lady Fortis bolted and, when we followed, Webb tried to block us again outside the front door. That was when DI Green finally lost patience and shot him in the leg. We all managed to tread on him at least once as we ran after her ladyship. Trouble was you got to her first.'

'But I couldn't have — '

'OK, Jack, you're not on trial. In fact I've a token of appreciation for you.' My raised eyebrows hurt my head. 'Here,' said Jim, putting a misshapen lump of metal in my hand. 'The bullet I was supposed to find, remember?'

'Oh — yes.'

'The irony is that we *did* find a bullet and it did come from the Armalite damaged in the crematorium fire. Seems at least one of your hunches was right.'

'Unbeliever,' I said, smugly. I stuffed the bullet under my pillows. Momentarily, I wished I could like him. 'How are the rest of the injured?' I asked.

'A few bruises and hurt pride. The local woodentops are put out they couldn't handle Webb in front of us visitors — and especially a woman visitor.'

'And how is she?'

'Ask her,' said Jim, standing up. 'He's all yours, ma'am. Cheers, Jack. Enjoy a rest while you can get it.'

Turning my head slowly, it still made me dizzy to move quickly, I saw her standing in the doorway. She was wearing the blonde wig and that green and gold dress she had worn in the garden of the Wheatsheaf the day the stone fell.

She sat on the chair next to my bed, looked solemnly at me, made no attempt to touch me. We listened to Jim Douglas walking away down the corridor.

'For you, Jack,' she said, putting two paperbacks on the bedside cabinet. 'Durrell and Eliot.'

'Thank you, Susie. Lovely choice.'

'Glad you're pleased.' A long silence while she didn't ask me how I was and I didn't tell her. Then we both began to smile.

'Good team, ain't we?' I said, cockily.

'In most respects,' she said, naughtily. 'But it was a pity Lady Fortis didn't spill the beans to me in the library. We've a lot of egg on our faces.'

'Life,' I said. 'Old man Frimmer was a bit spicy when he came to see me. Not only was he narked about the deaths he also rather wanted to claim obviousness. I pointed out that murder committed by prospective lover misled by incestuous son, followed by suicide of same prospective and deceived lover is not a particularly *obvious* scenario when you've only got accidental death by Dobermanns to start with.

'But I don't expect any real kicks. Frimmer's gone to the PM with two lots of good news. On the one hand everything's been cleaned up with minimum fuss and embarrassment for the government, on the other hand it wasn't a security issue at all — apart from the nonsense with the guns.'

'Well, I'm glad you're chirpy,' said Susie. 'Others aren't, especially in Testem Magna. Brad Ashmore was pretty shattered by the outcome; made it clear he wouldn't want to work with the likes of us again. Others in the village don't know whether to mourn the loss of business from The Hall or rejoice on the mountain of gossip. They're especially intrigued about you and me, but Ashmore and colleagues have been ordered to stick with the story we are archaeologists unfortunately caught up in a tragic accident.'

'Ashmore's playing ball?'

'Oh, yes. There's promotion in the air. But he's still upset that he will never know for certain whether Hardwicke or Nicky Stapolous took that shot at him. He's working off some of his irritation on the Wentalls: preaching sermons about gossip turning people into accessories to crimes. I think the whole village is in a general state of *brouhaha.*'

'Not surprised. We must've given 'em the most excitement since sliced bread.'

'I won't quote you on that in my report, Jack, but I do need to deal with your other views on the case before I start writing my fair copy.'

'Right. I've had time to collect my thoughts lying here. This is how I see it all.

'I believe Lady Fortis had lived for some time with a terrible suspicion of her son. Maybe it was fed by the growing horror of their relationship. What does it do to a mother caught in that incestuous, never-ending embrace? No chance ever to deny, ever to find another way of being. Ugh. I wonder if that was the reason her husband's study was kept exactly as it used to be. Obviously not a shrine, she didn't care for him enough for that to be the explanation. Perhaps it was the only gesture available to her in the face of her son's passion. Perhaps it reminded her she had once been capable of legitimate relationships with men. Perhaps, perhaps! Dear God, what we'll never know! And maybe she also felt it to be a denial of her growing conviction Nicky was somehow involved in her husband's death.'

'You think she was *not* party to that?'

'Yes, Susie, but can't prove it. I believe that Nicky's increasing instability, our arrival, Barnard Hardwicke's suicide, may have convinced her that her son was a murderer. We'll never prove that either, but it fits with her odd decision to come to the Wheatsheaf to meet us; almost as though she came to consult an oracle. And then the stone fell. Had she not been so troubled, so alarmed by events, she could have told James to drive her back home when Nicky said she wasn't to wait outside the police house. James could easily have returned later to pick him up.'

'So you see her as innocent?'

'Oh, no. My God, no! She spun the web that snared all the three men, used the power of her sex to make them demented. I'm not sorry I couldn't get out of the pool in time. You realize the possibility of her getting off had she lived? We just do not have the proofs with which to charge her.'

'And Nicky?'

'That bastard. I keep getting pictures of him, carrying his silly specially modified gun, going shooting with his stepfather and Hardwicke. If the older men's hair ever stood on end they probably associated the reaction with the slaughter of pheasants, not with Nicky scheming their deaths.'

'*Their* deaths?'

'Likely. He stumbled on a way to fix his stepfather's career, but one result of that was Sir Gregory was home all the time. And by then Nicky *may* have been his mother's lover for something like two years. I reckon he worked out how to set up Hardwicke as killer and get rid of him as well. So, promising the vet he could have his mother — how sick that was — he engineered the murder. Almost perfect. It was killing the dogs that was risky. He knew he wouldn't be able to get close enough to be certain a shotgun would kill them. So, with remarkable appropriateness he used the gun he originally stole so his stepfather lost his job. When he returned to the death scene he never called in at the gun room but at some hiding place in the house or stables where he had kept that gun for some future purpose. For all we know Nicky may always have planned to do more than disgrace his stepfather.

'Then he turned his attention on Hardwicke, murderer of his stepfather and rival for his mother's affections. A few weeks later Hardwicke dropped into his hand like a ripe plum, came up to The Hall with a tale about the local copper making jokes about Dobermanns. Nicky really wound him up, then sent him away. Then, using the same rifle, he set up the fake attempt on PC Ashmore.'

'Fake?'

'Yes, Susie. It must've occurred to you. A man armed with an Armalite rifle missing his target at a range of certainly not more than a hundred yards, probably a good deal less?'

'It did cross my mind, but we're a bit

short on proof, aren't we?'

'What's that?' I asked, primly. We grinned at each other. She shook her head at me. 'Well,' I said, 'setting aside inconvenient details like proof I'll continue the tale. Nicky knew he was in a position to squeeze Hardwicke. But there was just one thing he didn't know — and it's the greatest irony of all — he didn't know what his stepfather's job had been. He may have had some solid suspicions; after all it was probably the old boy's changed manner that caused Nicky to poke about in the first place: and he found guns. But Nicky never guessed how his stepfather's death had reverberated in Downing Street. The first intimation that he was out of his depth came when the shooting incident never appeared in the press. Then, a few weeks later, strangers appeared in the village. There was a young, brilliant, handsome archaeologist complete with incredibly luscious blonde assistant; a mysterious Mr Smith who vanished almost as soon as he arrived; a common, horsy-faced photographer who suddenly admitted to being a detective and moved in with PC Ashmore.

'Nicky did the only thing for which I admire him. He kept his head. He tightened the screws on Hardwicke and set up the second attempt on Ashmore — helped by us of course.'

'That reminds me, Jack. One of the few facts we've sorted is that Hardwicke was a keen motor-cyclist as a lad — until his mother made him give it up.'

'What that woman has to answer for! Anyway, Hardwicke was left holding the baby — two in fact — gun and bike. His only way out was to shop Nicky, but if he did that the murder of Sir Gregory would certainly come out. Even worse for Hardwicke was that he would be betraying the only son of the woman he loved. So he did what he could to prevent any trail leading to her and then killed himself.'

'Poor little sod.'

We sat silent for some time. 'It's a very persuasive theory,' she said at last.

'Ain't it?' I said, heavily sarcastic. She smiled at me.

'Now for the real — ' She paused. 'I nearly said 'the real world' then, as if the world of Testem Magna wasn't real.'

'Real enough,' I said. 'I think you're going to tell me about the world of expediency and wheeler-dealing.'

'True, Jack. So, in this other real world, this is how it is going to be. Sir Gregory died a horrible accidental death.'

'And Hardwicke's note?'

'What note?'

'I see, clever-clogs. And how's Ashmore been squared?'

'Frimmer's going to use muscle to make sure Brad goes to sergeant *and* can stay on in his beloved village, an arrangement not usually allowed. But Sergeant Ashmore will know that if ever there's a whisper of that note he will lose his stripes and be moved out of Testem.'

'Frimmer always did believe in firing off two barrels at a time.'

'True enough. And he's done exactly the same with Ashmore's Chief Constable. One barrel is national security, the other is threat of disgrace that his men didn't spot a murder on his own doorstep.'

'Right, Susie. So we have an accidental death and an inexplicable suicide. That's half the bodies accounted for. What's Frimmer doing about the other two corpses?'

'During routine inquiries about the theft of guns Nicky Stapolous suddenly tried to shoot the interviewing officer. The latter, returned fire, killed him. Mother, distraught, committed suicide before the wounded officer could restrain her.'

'And Fleet Street and inquests?'

'Don't worry. The PM's hit them with national security, issued D notices etc. He can use that ammunition just as effectively at top level as can Frimmer at our level.'

'Bet it isn't national security, Susie. Just political expediency. Not wanting to give the opposition any ammo.'

'Maybe. On the other hand if attention is refocused on Sir Gregory's family and on his death someone might get suspicious. That could lead to an interest in the civil servant who took over Sir Gregory's job.'

'He's probably a Russian anyway.'

'More than likely. Anyway, that's the PM's problem and, as you imply, it may be as much to do with an approaching election as with security.'

'So we've only Caliban to account for?'

'Caliban? Oh, yes, Jack. Our Mr Webb is returning to the service of the Arab sheikh he used to work for. In return for free medical treatment for his leg, dropping all charges, free air ticket, and a splendid gratuity in five years' time, James Webb will shortly take up a well paid domestic post in the Middle East. He knows that one of the effects of all that sunshine will be that memory fades.'

'So matters are closed or in hand?'

'Yes, Jack. Not a chance any of this stuff will ever come out in a courtroom. With all the principals dead it'd be a waste of time. And much as I like your theories, the Director of Public Prosecutions couldn't possibly accept them as a basis for bringing any charges even if there *was* anyone left alive to charge.'

'Absolutely, Susie. We can't even confirm motives.'

'I'm not sorry about that either. My sympathies are rather more with Lady Fortis than yours are.'

'Maybe so. Where does all this leave you?'

'OK I think. I've a bit of clearing up to do, finish the report etc. Also your role in the affair needs rewarding in some way, don't you think?'

'Nice way of putting it! Frimmer nearly had a stroke when he heard that another case involving me had not produced a major arrest, only casualties.'

'Nevertheless, he has agreed that your insightfulness and courage may be acknowledged in some way.'

'May be?'

'What would be the best celebration you could have?' Even as she asked her face began to change and my stomach began to churn. 'What do you say to a fortnight in Bermuda with me?'

I suppose there was *some* point in attempting to answer the question, but when the woman you most care about starts kissing you, you'd be a damned fool to start talking. As she pressed me back against my pillows I experienced a dull pain in my left buttock. I was also being pressed down on that misshapen lump of metal. Pain also is real.

We do hope that you have enjoyed reading this large print book.

Did you know that all of our titles are available for purchase?

We publish a wide range of high quality large print books including:
Romances, Mysteries, Classics
General Fiction
Non Fiction and Westerns

Special interest titles available in large print are:
The Little Oxford Dictionary
Music Book, Song Book
Hymn Book, Service Book

Also available from us courtesy of Oxford University Press:
Young Readers' Dictionary
(large print edition)
Young Readers' Thesaurus
(large print edition)

For further information or a free brochure, please contact us at:
Ulverscroft Large Print Books Ltd.,
The Green, Bradgate Road, Anstey,
Leicester, LE7 7FU, England.
Tel: (00 44) **0116 236 4325**
Fax: (00 44) **0116 234 0205**

Other titles in the
Linford Mystery Library:

CRADLE SNATCH

Peter Conway

Mr. Justice Craythorne is convinced that Janice Beaton is a wicked woman and sentences her to three years in prison — but later he is to discover just how wicked she is. After kidnapping the judge's baby grandson, she proceeds to terrorise his family . . . Cathy Weston leads the investigation but finds herself becoming emotionally involved with the baby's father. The physical and psychological pressures mount, and the young and vulnerable police inspector now finds herself targeted by Beaton and her sinister accomplice.

ODD WOMAN OUT

George Douglas

Chief Inspector Bill Hallam and sergeant 'Jack' Spratt of the Deniston C.I.D. are investigating the death of Madge Adkin. The dead woman had peculiar habits and claimed to be a bird-watcher, but knew nothing about birds. The trail they follow leads them to an escaped prisoner, an unorthodox 'healer' and a bunch of anonymous letters . . . The killer seems to have covered his tracks, but a blackmail attempt, quite unconnected with the murder, brings the detectives the proof they need.

CALLERS FOR DR. MORELLE

Ernest Dudley

In his Harley Street house, Dr. Morelle listens to Thelma Grayson describe how, the previous night, she had shot Ray Mercury. Thelma explains that Mercury had been responsible for her sister's suicide. The morning newspapers reported that Mercury had shot himself. Now, Thelma asks if she should give herself up to the police, or let them believe he shot himself? Morelle's search for the answer finds him and Miss Frayle adventuring into Soho's dark underworld, before finally trapping the murderer.